THE SAND BAR MISSTEP

A MCLAUGHLIN SISTERS NOVEL (STRANDED IN GETAWAY BAY ROMANCE, BOOK 4)

ELANA JOHNSON

ISBN-13: 978-1-63876-101-3

CHAPTER ONE

*I*vy McLaughlin bustled around the boutique, the new maxi-dress coverups tempting her. If she bought one, the money would come right out of her paycheck. She'd barely even miss it. Of course, she'd bought that crop top last week and a new pair of boyfriend jeans just yesterday. At the rate she was going, she'd be lucky to even get a paycheck on Friday.

So the swimming suit coverups went on the rack, despite her desire to take a size small in black to the dressing room and see how it looked with her newly bleached hair.

Everything about Ivy was new and improved. It had to be now that she was back on the market after a long relationship with Brooks Dentin—which had ended last week.

And she'd been so sure he'd asked her to the

fanciest fish house on the island to propose. But he'd gone all *Legally Blonde* on her and broken up with her. Ivy wasn't in a sorority, nor did she have any inclination to go to law school.

She just needed a new manicure. A new haircut and color. A new pair of jeans—*check*—and a new outlook on life.

Then she'd be fine.

Never mind that all of her sisters had now found love with some great guys. Eden and Holden were married now, as were Iris and Justin. Orchid and Maine would have an "event of the century" on the island by the end of the year, and Ivy was happy for all of them.

Honestly, she was.

She just wanted her own knight in shining armor. Or a football helmet. Or a Navy SEAL uniform. Or whatever. Since she'd been dating Brooks so seriously, she hadn't been calling in favors like she usually did to keep her social calendar full.

And now that she had access to the starting quarterback of the Orcas, she found she didn't want him to set up a date for her.

She wasn't sure what that meant, as Ivy was usually the life of the party. The star of the show. The one who turned heads, who could flirt with anyone with a Y-chromosome, the one who never stayed in on the weekends.

Now, she didn't even *want* to go out.

She felt broken inside, and she had no idea what to do about it.

Her phone rang, and she swiped on the call from her sister. "Heya, Eden," she said. "How's life in the glass building?"

"Just grand," Eden said, an edge to her voice that Ivy usually didn't hear unless Eden had good news.

"What's up?" Ivy turned toward the door as a chime sounded and watched two women walk into the shop.

"I have some exciting news," Eden said.

Ivy knew what her sister was going to say before Eden's voice landed in her ears. "Holden and I are expecting."

So maybe Ivy hadn't put those exact words in that exact order. A shriek had already started building beneath her vocal chords, and she let it out for just a moment. There was nothing better than being an aunt.

"I'm so excited for you guys," she gushed as the women came closer. If her boss were here and found her talking on the phone while there were customers in the store, he'd be furious. "Look, I have to go, but I'll call you back as soon as I can."

"Okay," Eden said, and Ivy hung up.

She approached the women. "Hey, ladies. Can I help you find something today?"

"She needs a new bathing suit," the brunette said.

"I do not," the other woman said. She threw her friend a scandalous look and tucked her regular brown hair behind her ear.

"Something sexy," the brunette said without missing a beat.

"Shannon."

"What?" Shannon asked. "You do. She's going to meet a guy out on this deserted island, and she wants to look hot for him. *Hot.* H-O-T."

"Stop it," the other woman said, actually reaching up and covering Shannon's mouth with her hand. "Just a regular bathing suit. I like a solid color. Black or red—"

"A solid color?" Shannon gasped as if her friend had just committed a fashion crime. She flipped a few more hangers on the rack in front of her, which didn't even hold swimming suits.

"We have some great one-shoulder stuff back here," Ivy said, hoping to draw the friend away from Shannon. "I've got solids and stripes." She really wanted to hear more about this deserted island. Maybe there was a singles event going on she hadn't heard about.

She'd been out of the singles scene for so long now, and part of her didn't want to get resubmerged in it. But summer had just arrived in Getaway Bay, and that brought a lot of vacationers out to the beaches.

Not only that, but summer was the best time to meet a new man, and Ivy felt some of the scales she'd been carrying for a while fall from her eyes. She could find a new boyfriend. She could.

She just didn't want to.

The island had plenty to do in the summer, and as

she pulled a black suit off the rack and held it out to the woman, she asked, "Where are you going to meet this guy?"

"Haven't you heard?" Her blue-green eyes sparkled with a secret. "There's this *crazy* billionaire who's put out an Internet ad." She rolled her eyes like the very idea was stupid. And yet, she was going to buy a sexy swimming suit to meet him. "He bought an island, and—"

"A deserted island," Shannon inserted.

"A deserted island," the woman continued. "And he wants someone to come live on it with him for three months. See if they can fall in love." She sighed like it was the most romantic thing in the world.

Ivy's heart started pulsing in her chest. At first, the sensation felt strange, as she hadn't felt anything like this in a while. Even while dating Brooks these last few months—which should've been a dead giveaway to her that their relationship wasn't going to last.

"She'll try that teal bikini too," Shannon said, and Ivy got it down amidst protests from the other woman.

"Come on, Kari," Shannon finally said. "You're going to meet this guy on his island. You can't show up in Bermudas and a T-shirt with a popsicle on it." She all but shoved her friend into the dressing room, another fistful of very revealing swimming suits in her hand.

Ivy smiled at the pair of them, their banter and back-and-forth so much like hers and Iris's. A pang of missing hit her hard when she thought of her twin. No, they couldn't stay together forever, but Ivy had always been so close to Iris, and she had Justin now.

The retired Navy SEAL worked for an app company now, and Ivy wondered if maybe he knew some single guys she could go out with.

Nope, she told herself as she picked up her phone from the check-out counter. She wasn't going to ask for help to get a date. Not this time.

No, this time, she was going to look up this crazy billionaire who'd bought an island and put out an ad for a companion. After all, money could make up for a lot of things. Maybe even a little bit of mental instability.

―――

THAT EVENING, IVY SAT AT HER COMPUTER, the cursor blinking in the empty chat box in front of her. She'd read all about Mason Martin and his scheme to find someone to spend his life with.

His words, not Ivy's.

He claimed to be from Texas, and his proposition was clear. Come to Long Bar Island, about two hours south of Getaway Bay, and spend three months there with him. See if a love connection could be made.

The end.

He wouldn't be compensating anyone, and the only way he'd send out pictures was if someone messaged him and asked.

So Ivy sat in front of the chat box, ready to ask. Any time now. "Any minute," she muttered to herself. Beside her on the desk, the small guinea pig she sometimes took out and carried around with her lay curled into a ball.

If she went out to Long Bar Island, she'd have to figure out what to do with Tommy.

"He's a guinea pig," she told herself.

She'd been talking to herself all afternoon since looking up the email order bride scandal that had Getaway Bay in a twitter. She wouldn't miss anyone's birthday. She wouldn't miss Orchid's and Maine's wedding. And Eden had said she wasn't due until the first week of January.

Ivy had her job at the boutique, but honestly, it was exactly that—a job. Not a career. If things didn't work out with this Mason fellow, she'd come home and find something else to do.

She couldn't *believe* she was even considering this. There were singles cruises and beach parties right here on the island.

"Hello," she said as she typed out the words. "My name is Ivy McLaughlin. I've read your proposal, and I think I might be a good fit."

She read over the words again, and then again. She didn't want to ask for a picture of him right up front, though she could admit that looks were important to her. What if he was some sort of Quasimodo, and she didn't know it until her boat landed on the island?

"It's not all about what he looks like," she reminded herself, her hand hovering above the mouse, which already sat on the send button. She wondered how many people had sent him messages. Did he walk around the island? Maybe she could meet him that way.

Because this just felt ridiculous.

Her doorbell rang, and she jumped. Her knees hit the pull-out tray that held her keyboard, and her hand hit the mouse.

Moving quickly, she got up and hurried to the front door, adrenaline streaming through her now. "You ordered sausage and anchovies?" The guy standing on her porch with her pizza couldn't be more than sixteen.

"Yes." Ivy took the pizza from him and handed him the twenty-dollar bill on her front table. "Thanks."

"No problem, ma'am." He saluted—actually saluted her—and turned to leave. Disgust coated her insides.

"Ma'am." She was only thirty-one-years-old. She wasn't a ma'am. Was she? "It doesn't matter," she told herself as she took her food into the kitchen. "He was way too young for you."

Something beeped from her computer, and she turned toward it. The machine sat just outside of the kitchen, back toward the front door. Another beep sounded, and a box popped up as she watched.

"Oh, holy starfish," she said, abandoning the food as she sprinted back to the computer.

She'd sent her message to Mason Martin when

she'd been startled by the pizza delivery guy. And he was responding. With pictures.

He had dark hair and dark eyes, and he looked downright good enough to eat. His broad shoulders met Ivy's requirements, and she could only imagine what he'd look like out on an island with his shirt off.

"He's handsome," she murmured as another image came up. Another box ticked. Rich. Good-looking. So he wasn't Quasimodo. Hopefully, he wouldn't be the Beast either.

Most people want to see what I look like, he'd typed. *That's me. Mason Martin. I'm 35.*

Are you from the island? Ivy typed into the box, all thoughts of eating now gone, because this man was checking her dating requirement boxes faster than she could remember what they were.

CHAPTER TWO

Mason Martin sat at his computer, rapt. He didn't normally do anything like this, as he'd spent at least seventy percent of his life under the brutal Texas sun, on his father's ranch. Then his.

Now someone else's, as he'd finally sold Fox Hill Ranch a few months ago. He'd already made the move across the ocean, and he'd been in Getaway Bay for nine months now. Dating here was just as hard as it had been in the wilds of Texas.

Probably harder, as he sported quite the farmer's tan despite his efforts to even out his skin tone on the beaches here. Not only that, but a man in a cowboy hat here seemed to draw all the wrong kinds of attention.

So with some of the billions he'd received from the sale of his generational land, he'd bought an island.

Long Bar Island, to be exact, and it was basically a patch of sand and trees and vegetation that got submerged in the late autumn and winter months.

But in the summer, it was glorious, with that sparkling teal water he'd seen in movies. No running water, but he had a yacht he could equip with everything he needed to survive for a while.

Three months, to be exact.

Are you from the island?

A message from the woman who'd started the conversation finally popped up, and Mason's fingers trembled slightly. At least he hoped she was a woman. He knew the dangers of online chatting better than most, and he had no idea who was really on the other side of this conversation.

No, he typed out. *I'm from Texas.*

Texas?

He almost rolled his eyes. This woman was probably some over-suntanned blonde who was more interested in his island than she was in him.

"She's the only one who's messaged," he told himself as he typed out another response.

Yes, Texas. I was born and raised there. I've been in Getaway Bay for just over nine months.

What do you do here?

What did he do here? He had no idea how to answer that question. He didn't have to work. He'd done a few odd jobs for the cattle ranch on the west side of the island. He'd helped with a construction project for a wedding planning business.

Not much, he typed out, staring at the words. Could he really send those? Surely what he did for a living wasn't up for debate, not if he was really going to go out to his island for three months and hope to fall in love.

Foolishness squirreled through him, and he leaned away from the computer without sending his message.

I work at a boutique downtown, she said in her next text. It's not much, but I like it. And I get a discount on clothes.

Mason smiled at the words, though he wasn't sure if he wanted a high-maintenance woman who wanted to shop all the time.

"You don't know anything about her," he muttered to himself. He had a tendency to make quick judgements and even quicker decisions. This exercise was supposed to help with both of those things.

And it's more than an exercise, he reminded himself as he started erasing what he'd typed so he could say something else. He really did want to fall in love. Find someone to share his life with. He'd been so lonely at the ranch, and he'd felt good about coming to Getaway Bay, sure his life would change for the better.

But it had just been the same, with a different view in the morning.

Mason wasn't sure what to do about that, but he wasn't going to sit in his high-rise apartment building and watch people sunbathe on the sand below. Not anymore.

He wanted a woman to love? He could find one. His Internet ad had been generating a lot of buzz, especially about who he was and what he looked like. In fact, he'd lunched next to two women talking about him and his ad that very day.

I'm retired, he typed. So I have plenty of free time.

You retired at age thirty-five?

I sold my ranch in Texas to come here. Mason figured he could get some things out of the way up front. That way, if this woman wasn't going to work out, he could move on to the next.

If there was a next, which so far, there wasn't. *What's your name?* he asked.

Starfish! Her next message made him frown and smile at the same time, and that was pretty hard to do.

"Starfish?" he asked the empty apartment. He hated being alone, and he severely regretted leaving his corgis behind in Three Rivers. But he hadn't thought the ranch dogs would like the beach. In hindsight, he realized he should've brought them, as there were plenty of canines playing catch in the sand most of the time.

I can't believe I didn't tell you my name. It's Ivy McLaughlin. I'm 31, and I work at a boutique, and I have three sisters.

Mason didn't want to ask for a picture, but well, he wanted to see what she looked like. A rectangle popped up, and a moment later, a beautiful blonde appeared.

That's me at my sister's wedding last year.

Ivy was utterly gorgeous—and exactly the kind of woman Mason had dated before. He knew he shouldn't compare her to his last serious girlfriend, but he couldn't help it. This Ivy even looked a little bit like Anne-Marie.

His heart twisted in his chest. That woman had stolen enough from him, and he wasn't going to give her another second of his time. Another ounce of thought.

So, he typed. What do you think of my plan?

I'm a little fuzzy on the details.

It's simple, he wrote. I own the island. I own a yacht with all the supplies. We sail out there—it's two hours away—and we live there for three months. See if we can get along. Help each other survive. Share our lives.

He almost sighed, but he held himself together. Yes, he was a big, rough-and-tumble cowboy. But he was also just a man, and a very lonely one at that.

Do you have any family?

His fingers hurt almost as much as his head. He didn't want to play get-to-know-you over the computer. He could do that on the Getaway Bay Singles app if he wanted to. He didn't want to.

His impatience with the conversation surged, and he backed away from the computer. His temper wasn't the longest fuse he possessed, and he figured he could take a break for a minute.

That minute became an hour, and then the next day, and he still hadn't answered Ivy. She hadn't messaged him again either, and Mason checked his ad to make sure it was still up.

It was, and the hits on it had doubled. And yet, no one else had messaged. Why not? Was there literally no one on the island of Getaway Bay willing to try this experiment with him?

He'd heard the word *crazy* get thrown around down in the lines for smoothies and under the trees at the taco joint.

Another day passed, and still nothing. He could go out to the island alone. Take down his ad. Lick his wounds. Sell everything he'd bought here in Getaway Bay and move on.

The grocery delivery guy had just left when his computer made a noise like a ruler tapping a desk.

He hurried over to the desk to find a message from Ivy. His heart fell a little bit, though he wasn't sure why. *Mason? Are you still here?*

Yes.

I'm in if the offer still stands. When do we leave?

Mason looked to the stack of bottled water on his kitchen counter. *How fast can you be ready?*

Depends on the packing list.

I'll bring everything we need. His fingers flew over the keyboard now, excitement building in his chest. *Food, water, supplies. We'll have my yacht too. You just need clothes and toiletries for three months.*

Will we be doing laundry?

Sure. He looked at the cursor, just blinking so merrily on the screen. *By hand.*

I can be ready whenever.

Let's say Monday, he typed. That was four days from now. Then she could say goodbye. Have a chance to buy anything she needed. The timeline also gave her time to back out, and Mason wasn't sure if he wanted her to or not.

She seemed nice, and she was beautiful. It just seemed so strange that no one else—not one single other person—had messaged him. Not even to see what he looked like.

Out of the forty thousand hits his ad had, he'd expected more than one brave soul to contact him.

Meet at the dock at ten?

See you then, she messaged, a row of smiley faces following the words.

Mason leaned away from the computer, hoping he wasn't getting pranked. But he didn't have a clue who would want to play a trick on him. His two older brothers ran the other half of the family ranching empire—a second, much larger ranch just north of Hill Country. He'd taken on the smaller—but still impressive—ranch in Three Rivers, up in the Texas Panhandle.

Their father had died four years ago, and their mother had chosen to live at Ramble Ridge with Elliott and Donald. They were both married. They both had children. They got along great, and Mason did too.

But he was the sore thumb, the one that stuck out, the one that didn't conform.

He'd tried. Honestly, he had.

He knew he wasn't perfect, but who was?

"Monday," he said to himself, and he suddenly had so very much to do to be ready to launch for Long Bar Island in just four days.

CHAPTER THREE

"*I*'ll be back in loads of time," Ivy said, her voice just a little whinier than she'd like it to be. "You won't have your baby by September." She aimed those words at Eden, who'd been salty about the idea of Ivy going out to Long Bar Island with a complete stranger from the moment Ivy had started speaking.

"And you won't be married by September." She looked at Orchid, hoping to get her oldest sister on her side, and stat.

Even Iris's mouth had dropped open after Ivy's proclamation that she'd met a man online and would be joining him for a survival expedition and a hopeful love connection on his private island.

Maybe she shouldn't have used the words "love connection." She wasn't sure.

"I can't believe you *want* to do this," Iris said. "I

almost *died* on a deserted island." She glanced at Justin, who wore a hard look on his face. "*We* almost died."

"He has a yacht filled with supplies," Ivy said. Honestly, she'd said that already. She hated it when no one listened to her.

"There are no spas on deserted islands," her father said.

"Dad." Ivy rolled her eyes. "Orchid?"

"Hey, we had a garden," Orchid said. "So our food situation wasn't terrible. It was more like I couldn't wash my hair. Or my clothes. Or you know, have any privacy for...private things."

"Again, he has a yacht," Ivy said. "I really think you guys are overreacting."

"And *I* really don't think you've thought this through," Eden said.

"Will you please pack me a backpack of supplies like you did for Orchid?" Ivy folded her arms. She was thirty-one-years-old, and she could go wherever she wanted, whenever she wanted, with whoever she wanted. She didn't need her mother's permission or Eden's blessing.

She would, however, like a backpack of supplies.

"When are you leaving?" Eden asked, pinching the bridge of her nose.

"Monday."

"I'll come over on Sunday." She stood up, Holden going with her. "I can't believe you want to do this."

"Honey." Iris stepped into them as well. "Brooks will come back to you. Begging, he'll come."

Ivy shook her head. "This isn't about Brooks."

Eden and Iris exchanged a glance that only made Ivy's fury rear its ugly head. "Right," Eden said.

"It's not," Ivy insisted. "He can do what he wants. I'll do what I want."

"And this is what you want?" Her father stood too, and Ivy met his eye.

"I want...okay, so I'm not exactly sure what I want. But I know I don't want to keep going into the boutique day after day. Selling a pair of overpriced flip flops or hanging up beachwear no one needs. I want to *do something*. I want to get out there and experience life."

"Take a cruise," Orchid said. "The singles cruises are really fun."

"Minus the tropical storms and tsunamis," Ivy said.

Orchid grinned at her. "Right. Minus those."

Tesla burst in the back door, a big white dog behind her. Her laughter filled the house, and Ivy stepped over to her niece. "I'll miss you so much."

Tesla giggled into Ivy's embrace, but she didn't ask where she was going. She hugged each of her family members, and Iris held onto her the longest. "Promise me you'll keep in touch."

"How do you think I'll do that?" Ivy asked.

"Eden's got a solar panel that charges phones," she said. "Right, Eden?"

"I'll put it in the pack," their most practical sister said, her voice almost a deadpan.

"You'll take Tommy?" she asked Iris.

"Who's Tommy?" Justin asked. "Because if he's as big as that dog of Tesla's, the answer is no."

"He's a guinea pig," Ivy said, smiling at her brother-in-law. "He's tiny, and he's silent, and you won't even know he's there."

"Sold." Justin gathered Ivy into a hug too, and he whispered, "If this guy isn't for you, don't be afraid to come home early, okay?"

She nodded into his shoulder, glad she had a few people in her corner. In reality, Ivy had the support of her whole family, and she knew it. She sniffed back her tears and went to start packing Tommy's things so he could go home with her twin.

MONDAY MORNING CAME SO QUICKLY, AND ALL of her sisters gathered one more time to see her off. She'd cried once already that morning, and she pulled over before the last turn that would get her to the dock to refresh her makeup.

After all, she only got one chance to make a first impression, and this guy was rich. She'd never envisioned herself with a cowboy, but then again, there were so few cowboys here in Getaway Bay.

And he was a retired cowboy, which meant he had to be something else now. At least in Ivy's mind.

With her best face painted on, she finished the drive to the dock, easily finding a huge yacht waiting down where the larger boats were usually tied. That thing had cost a pretty penny, and Ivy's excitement grew.

She parked next to a hulking, black SUV and got out of her car. Surely she couldn't leave her car here for the next ninety days, but she hadn't been given any direction on that. After popping her trunk, she pulled out her baggage, lining it all up on the asphalt near the back of the car.

"You must be Ivy."

She turned toward the male voice, ready to see Mason standing there. It wasn't him, but a tall, polished man in a suit. "Mister Martin is waiting for you on the yacht." He surveyed the bags Ivy had lined up. "You need all of these?"

"Yes," she said simply.

"Give me a moment, please." The butler stepped away and lifted a phone to his ear. He had the ability to speak so low that Ivy couldn't understand him, though he only stood a few feet from her.

"I'm sorry," he said, his words dripping with apology. "But Mister Martin says you only get two bags onboard *Starlight*."

"Two bags?" Ivy looked at the five on the ground in front of her. And the backpack hanging on her shoulder. "Surely this one doesn't count." She handed him the backpack. He held it in his hands like he might get a disease from touching it.

She'd already packed light. She'd be gone for three months. Three. *Months*. That took a lot of clothing and supplies. She opened her two biggest bags and started combing through them, making a pile on the ground as sweat poured down her face.

She stuffed as much as possible into the first bag and stood up, her back kinking from the position she'd been in for several long minutes.

"There." She heaved the bag to her right, a grunt following, along with a groan. "Sorry." Sweaty and annoyed, she swiped her hair out of her eyes, words bubbling against the back of her throat. Words about how this butler could've helped her or hey, wasn't there room for four bags on a ninety-foot yacht?

Come on. Was his precious *Starlight* too weak to carry her baggage? That yacht was *huge*.

But it wasn't the butler she'd hit.

"Mason," she said, stunned by his height, the breadth of his shoulders, the way he looked more CIA in those shades than almost anything.

He definitely wasn't a cowboy.

He stooped and picked up something from the ground. A cowboy hat. With that settled on his head, Ivy's definition of what made a man sexy and desirable shifted to a whole new level. She'd never date another man who didn't wear a cowboy hat. Ever.

Paired with the sunglasses and the gray tank top

and the blue board shorts…Ivy couldn't even remember what she was doing there.

"You can bring it all," he said smoothly.

"That guy said I only got two bags."

"I didn't realize what we were talking about." Mason looked down at the pile still on the asphalt. He bent to start putting it back in the suitcase at the same time Ivy did, and she dang near collided with him.

"Sorry," she said again, her balance completely off-kilter now. She knew she was going down, but she grabbed onto his bicep as a last-ditch effort to keep herself upright.

That didn't work, and she ended up pulling him down with her. Humiliation dove through her, and everything felt ten times hotter than it had already been.

"Sorry," she said one more time, wondering if she could ever live down the last three minutes of her life.

He grunted, a blip of annoyance in his expression, before he rolled away from her and onto his knees. The butler helped him stand, and Mason brushed his hands along his clothes while the butler helped her up too.

She exhaled heavily, a set of tears threatening to appear at any moment. She had no idea what to say or what to do.

"Henley," Mason said quietly, and the butler made short work of repacking her belongings and loading them onto a cart. As he pushed it toward the yacht, Ivy finally summoned the courage to look at the handsome cowboy billionaire slash beach movie star. Or whatever this guy was.

If she'd have met him on the beach, she'd have tried to get his number. Or at a concert. Or along the boardwalk. Something told her she would've never found him at any of those places, and she bent to pick up her backpack when he remained silent too.

"Can I leave my car here?"

"Henley will park it in my storage unit," Mason said, his voice round and smooth, with a definite cowboy twang in it. So he had money, but he wasn't super refined. Ivy liked that. She handed him her car keys, and they started toward the yacht too.

"Are you ready for this?" Mason asked as they approached the walkway that would take them onto the yacht.

Ivy paused at the same time he did. He passed her keys to Henley, and then Mason faced the yacht too.

"I think so," she said, her stomach more jittery than she would like. She told herself it was because she hadn't been out with a man as intriguing as Mason in a long time, but she somehow thought it was more than that.

Hitching the backpack full of emergency survival supplies higher onto her shoulder, she took the first step that would lead her onto the yacht.

Mason followed right behind her, and Ivy couldn't turn back even if she wanted to. He worked the ropes with the confidence of an expert, and then the yacht bobbed on her own in the water.

There's no turning back now, Ivy thought, her stomach clashing against itself the same way the waves did when they hit the cliffs.

CHAPTER FOUR

"You can join me at the helm, if you'd like." Mason met Ivy's gaze, and he could appreciate her beauty. Watching her unpack her clothes and then repack them had almost been comical. Getting hit with her extra-heavy luggage had not been.

She nodded, those clear, blue eyes full of apprehension. Mason put a smile on his face and headed for the bridge. He loved sailing, and that was one bright spot in his time on the island of Getaway Bay.

"This thing is huge," she said.

"Yeah," Mason agreed. "It's basically a really nice house on the water."

"Will I get a tour later?" Ivy asked.

"Of course," he said. "It's only a couple of hours to the island, though."

"Hmm." She faced the windows while he stepped over to the controls. The yacht had a captain's wheel, but he didn't use it to steer.

"Once we get away from the island, we can just set the steering." He wasn't sure why he was still talking. Most women made him nervous, especially blondes without cowgirl boots or tiny shorts.

Ivy wore more sophisticated clothes, and her white shorts extended halfway down her thigh. Just enough to tease him, but definitely more modest than the women he'd dated at the dancehalls in Texas.

She'd paired the shorts with silver sandals and a pale blue tank top that barely covered her bra straps. Mason yanked his eyes from her tan skin—no farmer's tan for her—and looked back out the windshield.

The bay would be busy, as it was now fully June and the vacationers seemed to have arrived in droves. His neighbors had told him they would, and they'd been right.

"Did you not like being a cowboy?" Ivy asked, turning toward Mason again.

"I loved it," he said.

"Then why did you sell your ranch?"

His mouth tightened into a line. He hadn't antici-pated spilling his guts in the first twenty minutes they were together. "Uh, things weren't working out there."

Ivy's gaze on the side of his face felt like laser beams, but he didn't look at her.

Several moments of silence went by. Mason scrambled for something to say, but he couldn't come up with anything. "Does Henley work for you?" she finally asked, a hint of frustration in her voice.

"Yes," he said. "He came with the apartment building."

"You bought an entire apartment building?"

"No." Mason shook his head, flustered. He couldn't drive the yacht and talk at the same time. "I mean, he's the doorman at the apartment building. The concierge. He's the concierge. We can hire him for things if we need him." He cut a glance at Ivy, and she seemed cool as a cucumber.

"Did you—?"

"Can we take a break from Twenty Questions?" he asked.

Ivy blinked, actually shrinking away from him. "Sure." She turned and reached for the door handle. "I'll take a tour myself."

"Ivy, wait."

But she didn't wait, and Mason sighed as the door hissed closed. He'd paid a pretty penny for this yacht, and he wasn't even sure he'd explored all the cabins yet. Ivy seemed like the kind of woman to enjoy the luxury, and he decided he'd give her a few minutes to herself.

He desperately needed a few for himself, which made absolutely no sense. He'd been alone for months and months, barely talking to anyone in the time he'd been on the island. And he'd put out his ad specifically to *get* someone to talk to.

"Scared her off already." He shook his head, Anne-Marie's words floating through his mind. *You're like the Beast, Mase. Someone gets close, and you snap at them.*

She'd gotten the closest, but in the end, she'd broken up with him too.

Maybe his bark was too loud, but he'd never actually bitten anyone.

Fifteen minutes later, he was free of all the traffic in the bay. He programmed in the coordinates for Long Bar Island and drew in a deep breath.

He found Ivy at the back of the boat, leaning up against the railing as the wind whipped through her hair. She looked like a vision from heaven, and Mason took a few moments to admire her.

"I can feel you staring at me." She turned and looked over her shoulder, a small smile on those full lips.

"Sorry," he said, taking a few steps forward and joining her. "And sorry about that in there. I was…." He exhaled heavily. "I sold my ranch in Texas, because my girlfriend." He cleared his throat. "My *fiancée* broke up with me, and I couldn't imagine living there without her."

"Oh, wow," Ivy said. "I'm so sorry. I didn't know."

"Of course you didn't." Mason flashed a smile in her direction, not truly looking at her. "Anyway, I was just a little flustered, and I didn't mean to snap at you."

She nodded and refocused on the horizon. "Do you like the ocean?"

"Love it," he said. "I was ranching up in the panhandle of Texas. There's not water like this there."

"I bet not." Ivy put off a good air, and Mason basked in the warmth of the sunshine and the vibrations of the boat moving beneath him.

"Did you take a look around?" he asked.

"A little," she said. "I've never been on a yacht before."

"Really? A woman like you?" He chuckled and leaned his elbows against the railing as he bent down. "I find that hard to believe."

"A woman like me?"

Mason heard the acid in her tone, and he whipped his attention to her. His heart pounded in the back of his throat, and the cutting glare on her face only accelerated it.

"What does that mean?" She folded her arms, and Mason may have been out of the dating pool for a while, but he knew what folded arms meant. Trouble.

"Nothing," he said quickly. "It just means...you're upscale."

"Upscale?"

How she could make that word sound undesirable, he wasn't sure.

"You're sophisticated," he hurried to explain. "More

so than the other women I've dated. That's all. It's good, I swear."

Ivy narrowed her eyes as if she could detect a lie just by squinting. Mason felt one breath away from complete failure. He'd already accumulated two strikes. Would a third blunder have Ivy pulling the plug on this survival experiment?

Surprisingly, Mason didn't want her to. He was surprised she'd shown up, and he was sure she had plenty of sob stories about her past, same as him. Otherwise, why would she be here?

"How many women answered your ad?" she asked.

Before he could answer, the yacht lurched, taking Mason's stomach with it. "Hold that thought," he said, turning and dashing back to the bridge. Ivy followed, arriving several seconds after him.

"What is it?"

"Nothing," he said. "I just needed to adjust the parameters on the speed."

"You're sure?" She looked around wildly as if they'd sink at any moment.

Mason watched her, felt the panic rolling from her. "Yes," he said slowly. "Everything is fine."

She wouldn't settle, and she didn't look at him.

"Hey," he said, reaching up to touch her face. He guided her gaze to his. "Look at me. We're fine. Everything's fine."

Ivy visibly calmed right before his eyes, and she even leaned into his touch. "Okay."

"You okay?" he asked.

"Yes," she said, stepping back so his hand would fall from her face. He tucked it into his pocket and continued to watch her.

"All of my sisters have been stranded," she finally said. "Two of them on deserted islands after ship malfunctions."

"Holy cow."

Ivy smiled and shrugged, the scales of her fear disappearing. "I'd say holy starfish, but yeah."

Starfish. She'd said it the other night too, on the chat. For some reason, it struck Mason as funny, and he started laughing. "Starfish," he repeated amidst the chuckles.

Ivy joined him, and finally all the ice between them was broken.

"There she is," he said, nodding toward the smudge on the horizon. "Long Bar Island."

After he'd righted the yacht, he and Ivy had settled near the front of the ship, on one of the outdoor dining decks. Mason wasn't overly stuffy, and he poured soda and served crackers to help keep the conversation flowing.

"I don't see it," Ivy said, shading her eyes with her hand.

"It's not huge," he said. "Probably forty square

miles. I've been out a few times." He tried not to let the pride seep into his voice.

"Is there—what's on the island?" Ivy turned toward him, but he couldn't see her eyes through the mirrored sunglasses. Since she'd put them on, Mason had found it easier to talk to her, and he had no idea what that meant.

"I built a little cabin," he said.

"Running water?"

He almost scoffed but pulled the sound back inside his throat. "No." He hooked his thumb behind them. "I brought a bunch of bottled water."

Ivy nodded, folding her arms across her middle. Her nerves lifted into the air around them, and Mason let them infect him too. Suddenly, his idea of living on this island with a woman sounded utterly ridiculous.

That was probably why he'd had exactly one person message him about it. Everyone else thought it was a joke.

"Oh, I see it," Ivy said, excitement coloring her words now. "It really is small." She glanced at him. "If we were stuck out here and no one knew it, that island would be very hard to find."

"Probably," Mason said, noting her worry. "But we're not stuck out here, and people do know where we are."

Ivy nodded, but she didn't unclench her arms. Mason left her standing on the bow and went to guide the ship exactly where he wanted it. He had to park quite far from the shore, as the water wasn't deep enough to house the yacht closer to the sand. Long Bar Island had a hook on the south end with some higher rocks, and the water was decently deep there.

He stopped the yacht and dropped the anchor, the sheer enormity of tasks ahead of them overwhelming him. He'd need to make probably six trips back and forth from the yacht to the island to get the supplies and food they needed. And all of Ivy's luggage. The bedding. All of it.

His stomach rumbled, and he stepped away from the bridge to call to Ivy. She walked toward him, and she said, "Tell me what to do to help."

Mason smiled at her, an intense attraction moving through him that he didn't understand. He just knew he liked that she'd volunteered to help. To work. She may be petite and blonde, but Mason liked that she wasn't going to treat this like a vacation.

"I was thinking we could have lunch first," he said. "It's just past noon, and then we'll have all afternoon to get the island set up." He lifted his eyebrows. "What do you think?"

Ivy took a moment to answer, and then she said, "Okay. Lunch sounds great."

"Great," Mason said, gesturing toward the door that led inside. "I'm not great in the kitchen, but I can make grilled cheese sandwiches."

"I hope you didn't only bring cheese," she said,

pushing her sunglasses up to rest on the top of her head.

"There's more than cheese," he assured her, thinking maybe she would be high-maintenance.

"Great," she said, moving in front of him. "Because I'm lactose intolerant."

CHAPTER FIVE

*I*vy listened for Mason's reaction behind her. Sure enough, a scoff came, albeit soft. "Really?" he asked.

"No," she said with a giggle. She turned back to him and took a step backward, then another one. "Just wanted to see what you'd say."

An adorable smile lit up his face, and he ducked his head, that cowboy hat covering his eyes. But Ivy had seen them, and they were dark and dreamy and delicious. Things hadn't started well, but Ivy never judged a relationship on the first date.

She'd known this guy for a couple of hours now, and this lunch would move them into second date territory.

She glanced around at the high-end finishes of the yacht. "This is so nice," she said, her eyes finding luxury everywhere she looked. "Dining for eight. Wow."

"Twelve, if I pull out the middle section," he said, almost as if he'd memorized the owner's manual for this yacht. "There are five cabins, each with their own bathroom." He stepped into the kitchen and set a pan on one of the burners.

Everything about this vessel intrigued Ivy, and she wandered past the table to a beautiful seating area, complete with a huge flat-screen TV. "Will we have any days where we hang out on the yacht?"

"I have no plans for our time on the island," Mason said, his voice slightly muffled.

Ivy glanced back toward the kitchen, but she couldn't see him. The words from the ad ran through her head. *Billionaire seeking companion to live on Long Bar Island for three months. Possible love connection wanted.*

Possible.

Ivy's feelings still stung slightly from when he'd asked her to stop asking questions. She wasn't sure how to get to know him if she didn't ask questions, and he certainly hadn't been asking. But he'd apologized quickly, and their conversation after that had been easy.

Of course, she'd mostly talked about her sisters and each of their stranded experiences. Mason had seemed interested, but he didn't add a whole lot to the conversation, and Ivy's throat stuck to itself it was so dry.

Behind her, Mason whistled while he worked, and

she found that simple action somehow comforting. With a quick glance over her shoulder, she ducked down the hall and explored the cabins on this level. Stairs led down, and there were more rooms down there.

The nicer ones—where Mason had obviously stayed previously—were on the main level, and Ivy returned there soon enough. Though she'd grown up in Getaway Bay, she hadn't spent a lot of time on a ship. There was something unsettling about them. Maybe the way they constantly moved. Or the fact that they could sink, trapping her beneath the water too.

She wasn't sure. No matter what it was, the seething need to get back to where she could see the sky drove her to return to the kitchen.

"There you are," Mason said.

"Yeah, I went exploring," she said, pulling out a chair from the dining room table and sitting down.

"Lunch is ready." He picked up two plates and brought them over to the table. Each had a grilled cheese sandwich on it, and he turned to grab a couple of bags of potato chips and more soda.

He grinned at Ivy as he sat down, and she wondered if she could ask him a question about himself now. Instead of trying that, she picked up her sandwich and took a bite. If he didn't want to answer questions, he should start the conversation.

He didn't. The more seconds passed, the more

uncomfortable Ivy became. It also became a game to her to see how long she could hold her tongue. The grilled cheese sandwich helped, as it was loaded with cheese and crispy and toasty on the outside.

He finished his sandwich and looked at her. "I suppose you want to know about my family."

"Sure," she said, practically shouting the word.

"I have a couple of brothers," he said. "They're older than me. They're both married and have kids. They work a ranch called Ramble Ridge. My mother lives there with them."

"Your family has two ranches?"

Mason's eyes hardened for a moment. "My father had four parcels of land at one point," he said carefully. "I inherited a...significant piece in Three Rivers. My brothers took over the main ranch when Dad passed away."

Ivy reached over and touched his hand. A shock moved through her, and she pulled away as if his skin had caught on fire. She wasn't sure what had just happened. Why she'd touched him at all. Her mind felt short-circuited, and all she could do was stare into Mason's eyes.

He softened right in front of her, and she caught a glimpse of the vulnerable cowboy he probably didn't let very many people see.

"I'm sorry," she said, her voice ragged around the edges. "Losing a parent has to be hard."

"My dad was...a rock." Mason sighed and looked

toward the sunlight coming in the windows. "I thought I was a born-and-bred cowboy. But the work became…work."

Ivy wasn't sure what that meant, but she nodded like she did. "So you left because ranching wasn't fun anymore? Or because of the girlfriend?"

"Both," he said, looking at her again. All of his shutters were back in place, carefully concealing how he really felt. Ivy liked a good challenge, and she mentally determined she'd figure this guy out.

"Should we go see this cabin you've built?" she asked, feeling flirtatious and ready to get off this boat.

"Sure," he said. "Bring the suitcase you need the most, as we'll have to go back and forth several times." He got up and started loading things—boxes of food and cases of water and heaps of supplies—near the back of the boat.

Ivy was pretty much useless, but she could carry what he told her to. She did that, and then he untied the lifeboat and got in it. It rocked all over the place, and nerves struck Ivy right behind the lungs.

She handed what she could to Mason, and he loaded the boat to the point that she thought it would sink.

"All right," he said. "Your turn." He extended his hand toward her, and she put her fingers in his. That delightful tingle started cruising along her skin. It crawled up to her elbow, then her shoulders, and his fingers tightened on hers.

"You have to step down, sweetheart," he said as if

he were talking to a spooked animal. Ivy thought she fit that bill pretty well, actually.

"I won't sink it?" she asked, her feet frozen to the deck.

"Nope. There's room for you right here." He indicated the bench he'd kept clear. "Come on now."

Ivy got herself to move, and Mason's hand gripped her with the power of a python. Next thing she knew, she stood in the boat, and he grinned at her like she'd just achieved something great.

He put those muscles to work, and they hit the sandy bottom only a few minutes later. He jumped out and pushed the boat the rest of the way out of the water, immediately unloading the boat.

Ivy moved a little slower, but she managed to get out of the boat without embarrassing herself. She picked up a box and followed Mason. Her shoes got tangled in the sand, and she kicked them off, marveling at the cabin in front of her.

It sat back off the beach, under the shade of some tall trees. Made of wood, the cabin wasn't anything to write home about, other than the fact that it existed on this tiny piece of land in the middle of so much water.

"This is so great," she told Mason after she'd walked inside. There were no rooms inside, but one big area with only a few pieces of furniture. Two cots. A long couch and a loveseat. Two straight-backed chairs, and a small, round table.

Mason put his boxes on the table, and said, "That one can go here too." He took it from her and surveyed the cabin. "It's not bad, right? I mean, it'll keep us dry when it rains. Keep the sun off our skin when we've had too much. Block the wind."

"It's great," she said, meeting his eyes. He wore some anxiety in his, and Ivy realized he'd worked hard on this cabin. He'd collected all of the supplies. Loaded the yacht. He'd done everything, and she'd shown up with four pieces of luggage.

"Thank you," she said, a hint of foolishness moving through her in the next moment. She turned away from him and walked back outside, intending to get something else from the boat. They worked in silence after that, bending, lifting, moving. He rowed them back to the yacht four times, and it seemed to take forever to get everything from the yacht to the island and where he wanted it.

Ivy didn't complain. She knew how to work hard, and she wanted him to know she could do anything he could.

Her back hurt, and she couldn't help thinking of the long inventory days she'd put in at the boutique. After a long day like that, she'd take a hot bath and order her favorite sushi. But there was no hot water on the island, and probably plenty of sushi—if she could catch it with her bare hands.

When it seemed like the work was finished, she

stood with the water lapping against her ankles, staring out into the expanse of the ocean. A powerful wave of missing hit her. She couldn't believe she'd left the main island, left her family.

She talked to one of them every single day, and tomorrow…she wouldn't.

"Hey." Mason stepped to her side, and Ivy instinctively leaned into him. "You okay?"

"Just thinking about my family."

He put his arm around her shoulders and it felt…nice.

"Do you miss your family?" she asked. "Hawaii is a long way from Texas."

"Not as much as you do, I think," he said, his voice barely louder than the wind and the waves as they sang nature's song together. "I lived at Fox Hill alone for quite a few years."

"Fox Hill. Is that the name of your ranch?"

"Yes," he said.

"And that's why you're not a big talker." She wasn't asking, so he couldn't get mad at her for asking too many questions.

"Am I not a big talker?" Mason asked, a false note of surprise in his voice.

Ivy laughed, the sound freeing and full. It chased away some of the lingering melancholy, and she tucked herself closer to Mason. "Not a big talker, no. But if you can whip us up some dinner, I'd be willing to forgive the silence."

A low chuckle started in Mason's chest, and Ivy liked the rumbling quality of it. So despite a rocky start, she thought she could stay on this island with this man —at least for one night.

CHAPTER SIX

*M*ason woke sometime in the middle of the night to a sound he wasn't quite sure about. He'd never actually slept on the island before, always electing to sleep on the yacht. He'd been out to Long Bar Island several times, of course. No one could build a cabin in a single day.

The high-pitched wail started again, and he sat up and looked across the cabin to the other cot. Ivy tossed and turned there, the cot also squeaking with the movement.

His first instinct was to wake her, comfort her. Standing on the beach with her earlier had been…nice. Simple. Sweet. Mason needed more of all three in his life, and he'd gone to bed with a grateful heart that she alone had answered his ad.

"Ivy?" he whispered into the darkness.

She quieted, and her breathing seemed just as

even as before. He settled back to sleep too, but it wasn't deep, and he never truly felt like he'd rested after that.

However, when he woke fully, Ivy's cot was empty, and the sunshine filled the cabin. He rubbed his hand through his hair and then across his eyes. He thought through what he needed to do that day and came up with…not much.

All of the supplies had been brought over from the yacht yesterday. He could sort through those this morning. But they had food and water. They had shelter. Since he wasn't much of a talker, he'd brought board games and puzzles, crossword puzzle books and several decks of cards.

He found Ivy outside, crouching down in front of the circle of stones he'd made yesterday for their fire pit. He hadn't actually started a fire though, and he'd made them sandwiches from the cold items he had in the best cooler money could buy.

But this morning, Ivy had a thin line of smoke coming up from the fire pit. Surprise and admiration moved through him as he crossed the sand to her. "You started a fire?"

"I thought I'd scramble eggs for breakfast," she said without looking at him. She coaxed the flame cupped beneath her hands to glow brighter, and Mason found her downright sexy in that moment.

With tousled hair and dirty hands, crouched over a baby spark and trying to get it to play nice with the tinder. She was so much more than he'd first given her credit for.

"One of my favorite foods is scrambled eggs," he said.

"Really?" she asked. "Out of all the foods there are?"

Mason shrugged. "My grandmother used to make them with sour cream." The memories slipped through his mind, bringing a smile to his soul. "And they were one of the very first things my mother let me cook by myself."

Ivy simply blew on the flame again, but it didn't catch. In fact, it went out. "Starfish," she said under her breath, and Mason liked that she could use the word in happy situations and frustrating ones.

"You've got to put the shavings by themselves," he said.

"I tried that," she said. "They burnt too quickly, and then the fire was gone before I could get anything else to catch."

"I can do it."

She lifted those blue eyes to look at him, and Mason almost stumbled backward from the flames she had in her gaze. "*I* can do it too."

"I didn't say you couldn't." Mason felt like he'd just been hollowed out with a single look and a few words.

"I don't need you to do everything for me," she said.

Mason frowned. "I never said that."

"Right." She twisted away from him, but the sarcasm in her last word wasn't lost on him.

"Hey," he said. "What's going on?"

"I heard you talking in your sleep." Ivy cut him a dirty look and went back to piling the shavings from the fire-starting kit. "And this box lies. This says 'Easy!' It's not easy."

Mason once again wanted to help her, but he kept his hands to himself. "What did I say in my sleep?"

"Something about how you didn't want me to mess anything up."

"How do you know I was talking about you?"

"You said, 'Ivy, don't touch that. Leave it alone. No, don't mess it up.'" She cocked one eyebrow at him and plucked a match from the book. He could see she'd already used several, and a blip of panic moved through him.

He did want to tell her not to mess this up. He didn't have unlimited matches, and it was only the second day.

"I don't even know what I was dreaming," he said. "Are you really going to be mad about something I said while I was asleep?"

"The mind always brings out our true thoughts while we sleep," she said, which Mason took as code for yes.

"How do you even know that?"

"I read it once."

Mason scoffed. "I don't think that's true."

The shavings caught the flame, and Ivy focused on the little pile in front of her, gently feeding it bigger pieces of fuel until the flames had truly caught on a piece of wood big enough to play for a while.

"I got it," she said, true shock in her voice. She looked at Mason, wonder in those blue eyes. "I did it."

"You did it," he said, smiling at her. "Now don't let it go out."

Her expression soured, and Mason sighed. Would he ever be able to say anything right? He apparently couldn't even do so while he slept.

With the fire going strong, they both straightened. Ivy looked at him with apprehension. "I do want you to know that I don't need to be babysat out here. I can take care of myself."

"Noted." He leaned toward her. "What if I *want* to take care of you?" He wasn't sure where the question had come from. He usually only said what had to be said, and maybe this was one of those times.

His pulse beat against his breastbone while he waited for her to respond. "Maybe I'm not the only non-talker." He grinned at her, tucked a loose piece of her hair behind her ear, and went to get the carton of eggs from the cooler.

She whipped up the eggs and cooked them right over the flame. The pride in her body language wasn't hard to read, and she smiled at him as she handed him a plate of his favorite food.

"My favorite food is hot chocolate," she said as

she sat next to him on the long log he'd dragged over next to the cabin. The fire danced merrily in front of them, and Mason let the relaxation move through him.

"I think that's a drink," he finally said. "Not a food."

"With marshmallows."

"Oh, now, there you go," he said. "Definitely a food."

"When Eden was stuck on Bald Cliff Mountain, I made hot chocolate by the gallon." She shook her head as a smile crept across her face. "No one drank it but me."

"It seems like an odd choice for a tropical location," Mason said, hoping he wouldn't offend her unknowingly again.

"Yes, well, we don't all have such practical favorites." She nudged him with her shoulder. "So what are we going to do all day? You don't talk, and I can't do anything."

"Ivy, I never said that."

"I know," she said, meeting his eye again. "I guess I am a little high-maintenance, and maybe I'm a little sensitive about it."

"High-maintenance in what way?" he asked.

"Oh, you know. I like shoes and clothes and getting my nails done."

Mason nodded, though all of those things sounded like his worst nightmare. As long as he didn't have to go to the salon or the mall, he should be fine. "I brought games and puzzles. We could start one of those."

"Okay." Ivy wanted to play outside, so Mason moved the table out to the sand, and they started flipping over pieces to make the city of Paris. Ivy started talking about her job, and then the pets she'd had growing up, and Mason just listened to the sound of her voice.

After an hour or so, he just needed to be alone. "I'll be back," he promised, and then he ducked into the foliage behind the cabin, the sound of silence worth all the gold in the world.

You like her though, he told himself as he moved down the path he'd created that led to the spring. And he did like her. He wasn't sure *he* was *her* type though, and he wondered if she'd last for the full three months on the island.

THE DAYS PASSED, AND BOREDOM BECAME THE thing Mason fought with the most. He didn't want to do another jigsaw puzzle. He couldn't care less about crossword puzzles. Ivy turned out to be very good at card games and board games and word games, and it was no fun losing to her over and over again.

The island wasn't that big, and he hadn't brought anything to work it with anyway. No shovel. No seeds. No saw to cut a tree down and whittle it into something useful. Not only that, but Ivy had started making a list of all the things it would be nice to have on the island, as if the groceries, cabin, and loads of bottled water weren't enough.

Every time Mason felt his temper ignite, he excused himself to take a walk around the island. He never went too terribly far, as forty square miles was more than what it sounded like. And he always returned in a better mood, ready to talk about something else. Fine, Ivy did most of the talking.

But she didn't seem to mind, and Mason didn't either. He told her about his brothers. His childhood. Nothing too revelatory in his past that needed to be discussed. She didn't mention anything either.

As another afternoon faded into evening, he laid on the sand next to her, their hands intertwined. She'd fallen silent, and Mason really liked the times like this. Time where he could hear himself think and feel the presence of another human being beside him.

"Ivy?" he asked, his voice really quiet.

"Mm?"

"I really like you."

She shifted next to him, but he kept his eyes closed and his body perfectly still. "I like you too, Mason." He heard the smile in her voice, and he let one drift across his face too.

"Are you glad you came?" he asked.

"You know what? I am." She shifted again, sliding right into his side. Both of her hands held his, and he liked the added warmth of her body beside his. The wind picked up, and the sun went behind a cloud.

The change caused Mason to open his eyes, and he looked up into the sky. Blinking, it took a few moments to process that things were darkening quickly.

"Something's wrong," he said, sitting up. Ivy came with him, and she sucked in a breath at the same time he did.

The snarling storm coming toward the island seemed to be moving at the speed of sound. When the first raindrops hit his skin, he said, "Get to the cabin, Ivy. Now."

CHAPTER SEVEN

*I*vy's heart sprinted in her chest as she ran toward the cabin. Mason arrived before her, but he waited for her to dash past him before he slammed the door. "Let's put the couch in front of it."

Panting, and with panic rolling through her, she helped Mason push the couch into the door. The wind slammed into the cabin in the next moment, and a yelp tore from her throat.

This wasn't a permanent structure. It might not even stand.

Something pounded on the roof, and Ivy cowered into Mason. "What's that?"

"Rain." Mason looked up too. At least nothing was dripping from the ceiling—yet.

Ivy took a breath. Then another. Everything seemed eerily quiet, and then something huge and hulking hit the cabin.

She screamed. Mason yelled. They both darted away from the couch where they'd been standing.

There was no bathroom here. No plumbing that went down into the ground. No help.

"The main support is back here," Mason said, taking her hand and leading her toward the back wall. He pulled the loveseat over and turned it so it was perpendicular to the wall. Then he hauled over the table and the chairs, creating a small shelter for the two of them to huddle in.

"In, in," he said, glancing over his shoulder. Ivy practically dove between the loveseat and the over-turned kitchen chairs, pulling one closer to her so she could cower under it if she had to. She didn't really fit, but Mason joined her, pulling his chair in as well.

He grabbed onto the table and pulled that into them as well, covering them and part of the loveseat with the tabletop.

Relief rushed through Ivy at the same time the ceiling got ripped off the cabin. A scream tore through her throat as the wind snaked its icy hand inside the cabin.

"It's okay," Mason said, yelling to be heard above the storm. The rain pounded on the table and the loveseat behind them. There was no way she was going to stay dry through this ordeal, and she clung to the chair legs, her fingers gripped so tight, so tight.

Noise filled the air that she couldn't make sense of, but beside her, Mason said, "The yacht."

All at once, the shrieking sounds in her ears made sense. They were metal. Metal being twisted in ways it shouldn't.

Her heart sank to her toes and rebounded back to her chest, settling in the wrong spot. The yacht. They were stuck on this island without that yacht. She couldn't shower without that yacht.

Orchid's warnings about how nice a hot shower was after only a few days ran through her mind, an utterly ridiculous thing to be thinking about given the circumstances.

They'd hauled in all the food, thankfully. The water. Their luggage. All of it was getting soaked, but Ivy put it out of her mind.

She had to survive this storm. Then figure out how to live with whatever Mother Nature left behind for them. For almost three months.

One, two, three.... She kept counting until she reached eight—the number of days they'd been on this island together.

Eight, seven, six.... She counted backward and then forward while the storm raged around her.

Every muscle felt stretched tight, and she wasn't sure how to get them to stop screaming.

All at once, as quickly as the storm had descended upon them, it passed over. Silence reigned, but Ivy didn't dare move.

She lifted her head to find Mason still bent over the chair. "I think it's passed," she said. Her voice sounded like a phantom of itself, and she suddenly understood why her sisters had changed so much after their experiences on deserted islands.

She couldn't even think straight, and her thoughts flew from one side of her mind to the other. "Come on," she said. "Let's go see what the damage is."

She leaned into the table and slid it over enough so she could stand and step over the chairs. The sky above her still held some ominous clouds, and rain peppered her face as she looked up.

The walls were still standing, and Ivy moved the big couch too to get to the door. "Everything we have is going to be wet," she said, expecting to find Mason behind her.

But he was still over by the loveseat. She returned to him. "Mason, come on. The storm is mostly past us."

He looked up at her, a glazed look in his eyes. Ivy had seen this shocked look before, and she bent down. "Hey," she said kindly. "It's fine. Let's go look around." She extended her hand toward him, and he took it.

She wasn't strong enough to pull him up, and he got himself on his feet. "That was like being in a tornado," he said. "I survived one of those as a boy." His voice came out lower than normal, definitely with more emotion than Ivy had heard in the week they'd spent together.

"Wow, a tornado," she said. "We have hurricanes here."

"Is that what that was?"

"I doubt it," she said, stepping toward the doorway. The door hung on by one hinge. Her heart ping-ponged around now, as she had no idea what to expect on the other side of the doorway. She stepped out enough that Mason could follow her, and together, they faced the water.

The waves crested and foamed with white tips, coming up the beach much farther than they had previously. Branches and palm fronds littered the beach.

But the biggest problem was the yacht.

It clearly drifted in the water, pressing closer and closer to the beach. "It's going to get stuck," she said. It was still a magnificent vessel, but the glass she'd looked out as Mason had steered them here was obviously shattered. One of the railings she could see was bent at an odd angle.

"I'll row out to it and see if I can anchor it," he said.

"I'm going with you." She stepped when he did, both of them seeming to realize at the same time that their lifeboat had disappeared. "Can we swim?" she asked.

"I guess we'll have to."

Ivy went with Mason, something new and painful opening up inside her chest. She'd never done anything of honor. No one cared that she knew which dresses were new or in style. Anyone could feed a guinea pig.

She knew she was a good sister and a good aunt and a good daughter, but as she waded into the water, she felt powerful in a way she never had before. She felt necessary. Needed.

And brave.

She didn't have to swim to reach the yacht, as it had beached itself far enough up the beach that the water only went to her chest. Every swell of the waves, though, and she bobbed up and then went under, so she was dripping with saltwater by the time she climbed on board *Starlight*.

She blew her breath out and wiped her hair out of her face. "Okay, that wasn't so bad."

Mason's mouth in that tight line didn't agree. He went inside where the dining room, kitchen, and living area was, and Ivy followed him. She didn't want to be alone right now for some reason, almost like the storm would return and sweep her off the face of the earth the way it had the lifeboat and the roof.

"Everything's wet," he said, looking around. He stepped over the burners he'd used to make their sandwiches and twisted the knobs. Nothing happened. "No power."

"The lower cabins would provide decent shelter," she said. "I mean, not if there's another storm like that. But if it starts raining a lot or we need to get out of the sun."

Mason said nothing. He just cast one more look around this large cabin and then went back outside. Frustration filled Ivy, but she went with him.

There was no power on the bridge, and the chain

that had held the anchor to the boat had snapped. He had no way to fix it, and they ended up returning to the island just a little wetter than they were before.

Ivy started picking up branches and palm fronds and making a pile. She didn't need to do it. She wasn't even sure why she was doing it. But the rain stopped while she worked, and the sun returned, and before she knew it, her clothes were dry, and her stomach wanted food. Now.

"I'll make sandwiches," she said as she passed Mason. He'd taken up residence on a spot on the beach and sat staring out at the water. She put together turkey and Swiss sandwiches just like he had that first night on the island.

She got a fire started. She put the kettle on it to make coffee. She collected twigs and dragged the branches closer to the firepit. Every so often, she'd cast a glance at Mason, and he never so much as moved. Other than to eat, which he probably did without knowing it.

Once the coffee finished brewing, she returned to Mason's side. "Hey," she said gently. She'd seen people in shock before. Her sister, for one, when her husband's yacht had sunk. They'd never recovered his body.

"Come sit by the fire," she said. "Have some coffee."

Mason turned his head toward her, blinking as if he

was realizing for the first time that he wasn't alone on Long Bar Island.

She offered him a smile, hoping he would snap out of whatever funk he'd fallen into. "Come on," she said, threading her fingers through his. He squeezed back, his eyes so dark underneath that cowboy hat.

He got up and followed her over to the fire. She poured him a cup of coffee and he curled his hands around the mug as if he were cold. "I'm sorry, Ivy," he said.

"Why?" she asked. "Because you can't control the weather?" She sat beside him on the log and sipped her coffee. "Maybe because this isn't hot chocolate."

Mason started to chuckle. The laughter grew and grew, and pride filled Ivy that she'd been able to affect him so strongly.

"I didn't get the memo about the hot chocolate," he said.

She leaned her head against his shoulder, and he lifted his arm around her. She snuggled into his side and said, "Next time."

CHAPTER EIGHT

Oh, there would be no next time. Mason couldn't *believe* he'd thought coming out here with a woman was a good idea. Of course, five hours ago, everything had been peaches and cream. Bright sun. Hot sand. Beautiful woman.

There weren't supposed to be any storms.

"What about our cell phones?" he asked, thoughts forming in his mind again. He'd lost himself for a while there. He wasn't even sure how long, only that he didn't remember Ivy building a fire or making coffee. He felt like he should be hungry, but he wasn't. She'd probably fed him, and he didn't even know it.

"We left them on the yacht," she said. "Remember? We agreed only to check in with our families once a week."

"Right," he said. "But things have changed." He stood up, ready to wade back into the water and get his phone. Call everyone he knew until he got word that a ship was on the way to rescue them.

"Mase," she said, and that made Mason freeze. He turned back to her, his heart thumping inside his chest. Only one person called him *Mase*, and that had been Anne-Marie, his ex-fiancée.

Ivy got up and walked toward him, nowhere near the same as Anne-Marie. She wasn't from Texas, for one. She was much kinder, for another. And while she was definitely frustrated with him, she wore a smile on her face.

"Are you okay?" she asked, putting her hands on his shoulders. "Because you seem a little out of it."

"I'm...I was out of it for a minute," he said.

"Yeah." She tucked her hair behind her ear. "What did you eat for lunch?"

"I have no idea." Embarrassment heated his face. "I think I slipped into some shock there."

"You sure did," she said. "So let's go slow, okay? If you want to go out to the yacht to check our phones, let's go." She continued out into the water, and Mason followed her. Getting back on the yacht was easy but seeing all the damage wasn't.

His heart hurt, as he'd loved this yacht. Loved sailing around Getaway Bay, just himself and all that water. The ocean breeze. Whatever soda he'd wanted that day.

"The phones aren't here," Ivy said, once again jolting him out of his own mind. He turned toward the kitchen, where they'd both left their phones in the top drawer near the refrigerator.

He joined her. "They have to be here."

"They're not." She pointed to the drawer.

"Was the drawer open?"

"Yes," she said.

Mason looked down to the ground, expecting to see the devices there. But there was nothing but dirty water. Frustration filled Mason from top to bottom as Ivy pulled open another drawer.

"They have to be here," he said. Did cell phones just float away? Surely they'd sink.

"Here's mine," she said, pulling it out from underneath the dripping rug he kept in front of the tiny sink. Water dripped from the corner of the phone, and Mason's heart sank.

"No way that will work."

She pushed buttons and held them down. "Nope. Nothing." Their eyes met, and time stilled for Mason.

"The radio was out," he whispered.

"People will come when we don't check in," she said. "They know where we are."

"We checked in yesterday," Mason said.

"It's six days," Ivy said as he left the kitchen. "Iris will send the Navy SEALs when I don't call her."

Mason believed Ivy, and they did have food. He liked Ivy, and a sense of calmness started to come over him, replacing the numbness and the panic.

"Okay," she said, pulling in a big breath after that. "We should—oh, look. There's your phone."

Mason turned as she plucked it from between the tines on the burner. A twangy melody filled the air, and Mason's heart took courage.

"It's turning on," Ivy said, her voice full of excitement. She handed him the phone, and Mason watched as it powered up. "Do you have service?"

"It's coming," he said.

"We can call." She grabbed onto his arm with both hands and laughed.

Mason lifted his eyes to hers, and everything around him fell away. "Thank you for…not freaking out," he said, reaching up to push her hair off her face.

In fact, he'd been the one who'd freaked out, while she'd been steady and calm in the face of the storm.

They'd survived. They had food and water and solid ground to stay on. They would be okay.

Ivy smiled up at him, cradling his face in one palm. She gazed at him with all the things he wanted to see in a woman's eyes, and his nerves went wild. His phone beeped, and he used that as a distraction.

He wanted to kiss Ivy. Badly. But he'd known her for such a short time, and he hadn't had a relationship in so long, and he wasn't sure if how he felt was real.

Feels real, he thought as he swiped and tapped. Ivy had checked in with her sisters for the past couple of weeks, but Mason had simply gone to his private bedroom and checked his email.

But no one really emailed him anymore. He could've called his brothers, but he hadn't. He had a couple of friends on the island, but no one he'd call once a week to discuss his love life or how things were going on the island.

He called Drake Summers, a man who lived down the road from him and worked out at the cattle ranch on the island. He'd tried to get Mason to take a job, but Mason hadn't wanted to jump into another ranch.

Texas held a special place in his heart, but Mason just needed a break.

The phone rang once, twice, three times, and then something crackled and sparked. He dropped his phone as fire touched his hand, and Ivy yelped as she jumped back.

The phone smoked, and the silence on the yacht meant the call had definitely disconnected.

Mason took a deep breath and walked away.

"Mason," Ivy called after him.

"I'm going to try the radio again," he said, leaving the dining area in favor of the sunshine. He went around to the bridge, though he'd been up here...well, he wasn't sure how long ago. Hours maybe.

Everything looked the same, and he flipped switches and turned knobs to no avail. Literally nothing happened, and Mason leaned both elbows against the counter and held his head in his hands.

When he heard footsteps, he straightened and

pulled himself together. "Let's head back," he said to Ivy with a smile.

"Are you sure you're okay?" she asked.

"I'm fine." He slipped his hand into hers and squeezed. "Let's go see what food and water we have, so we can ration."

"I don't think we need to ration," Ivy said. "Like I said, when I don't call Iris, she'll send out her husband's friends."

Mason nodded. "Okay," he said. "I still want to take an inventory." They waded back to the island, and Mason started cleaning up. Ivy dug in and got to work too, and soon enough, they had everything in piles. Branches. Palm fronds. Debris.

The food and water waited in the cabin that now had no roof, and Mason's head hurt. "Okay," he said. "We can do this. We'll still be able to sleep in the cabin, and we have enough water for the full three months."

"We're going to be fine." Ivy pulled her ponytail out and put it in again, tighter this time. Mason smiled at her, but he didn't believe her.

Six days until she should be checking in with her sister. If she didn't, how long would it take for Iris to get the SEALs deployed?

Maybe a day.

And Long Bar Island was only a couple of hours from Getaway Bay.

So eight days.

They definitely had enough food and water for eight

days, and he returned his attention to Ivy. His thoughts wandered down the romantic path, and he dropped his eyes to her lips.

Clearing his throat, he quickly looked away again. "Let's get back to the island."

THAT NIGHT, MASON LAY ON THE SAND, feeling exposed and alone. Ivy slept cuddled into him, and he tightened his hand on her arm, glad she could still tolerate him. He knew he was a bit prickly, especially if things didn't go his way.

He couldn't sleep though he was beyond exhausted. He prided himself on thinking of everything, right down to the last detail, and it bothered him that he hadn't anticipated a storm. Well, he had—he knew Hawaii had tropical storms and hurricanes—but there hadn't been anything in the forecast, and they'd only been on the island for a week.

He didn't like sleeping beneath such a huge sky, though he'd been born and raised in Texas, where everything was bigger than life itself. He'd never had a problem being alone on the ranch. Never minded being out on the range, without a roof over his head. Heaven knew he'd spent plenty of nights keeping his cows safe and eating out of a can.

He could definitely survive this. A twinge of guilt

stole through him that Ivy had to, though, as that hadn't been part of the deal.

Still, she'd come, and she'd lived on the island of Getaway Bay her whole life. She knew the weather couldn't be controlled. She, probably better than anyone else, as all of her sisters had suffered mishaps because of inclement weather.

With those thoughts in his head, he pressed his lips to her forehead and closed his eyes. Sleep finally came.

When he woke, it felt like he had just dozed off. But the sun shone brightly above the horizon, and Ivy said, "Good morning, cowboy," in her sexy, flirty voice.

She lifted her head from his embrace, a smile on those lips. Mason didn't hesitate this time. He cradled her face with one hand and brought his mouth to hers in a sweet kiss that made his head spin.

For a moment, he thought she'd push him away. Slap him back. Tell him it was too soon, that she barely knew him, that he had no right.

But she didn't do any of those things.

She melted right into his touch and kissed him back. Tingles erupted along his scalp as she dragged her fingers through his hair, and Mason couldn't believe this was happening.

He'd kissed other women before, of course. But no one for a while, and Anne-Marie had never kissed him with this level of enthusiasm.

Ivy finally pulled away, leaving Mason hungry for more. Instead, he pressed his lips together, tasting her there, and smiled. She giggled, the sound driving right into his heart. She rolled away from him with, "Coffee?"

"Yes," he called after her, rolling to watch her walk away from him. He honestly hadn't been sure about her the first time he'd seen her, bent over that suitcase and muttering about the clothes she could or couldn't bring.

She'd been slightly cold toward him, and he hadn't known how to talk to her. But he did now, and it had only been a week.

He sat up and watched the golden light as it played with the tips of the waves. Such a serene scene calmed him, and he couldn't believe that just twenty-four hours ago, everything had changed.

Ivy returned with a bottle of water and a cup of coffee and sat in the sand beside him. She sighed and said, "So what do you think? Are we making a love connection?"

CHAPTER NINE

*I*vy liked flirting with a handsome man, and she was very good at it. Mason was so different from any of the men she'd dated before. He wore a cowboy hat for one, and though he had plenty of money, like some of the other men she'd dated, he was completely different from anyone on the island.

It was almost like he didn't know he had money. But seriously, who was retired at age thirty-five?

"Um," he said.

She laughed, tipping her head back and letting the sound flow from her throat. "I'm teasing, Mason," she said. "Does anyone call you Mase?"

"Uh, only one person ever has," he said.

"The girlfriend."

"I asked her to marry me," Mason said. "That makes her a fiancée."

Ivy gazed out over the waves, wishing she could call Iris right now. She'd thought the missing would go away after a few days, but it only seemed to intensify. "I've never been engaged," she said.

"It's not all that exciting," he said. "At least for me, it wasn't."

"No?" Ivy looked at him, trying to see something he hadn't said. If there was anything the last eight days had taught her, it was that Mason Martin didn't waste words. If he had something to say, he said it. "If it wasn't exciting, I don't think you did it right."

"Are you saying I botched the proposal?"

"I have no idea," she said, enjoying this game. "Tell me how it went down."

"Oh, it's a boring story."

"Definitely did it wrong then."

"I took her to buy the ring herself. Anne-Marie was…quite particular," he said, his voice slipping down a little bit. "She loved the sound of her own voice, and she was extremely intelligent."

Ivy didn't know what to say to that. Mason wasn't a big talker, and she'd carried the conversation for days. But not because she loved the sound of her own voice. "You didn't say how you proposed."

"Yes, I did. I took her to buy the ring." Mason looked at her, and Ivy searched his face. "I can tell that would not be good enough for you."

Ivy shook her head, trying to hold her smile back. "I mean, I'd be fine."

"Liar." Mason started laughing, and he slipped one hand into hers and lifted his coffee to his lips with the other. He hadn't even swallowed yet when he spit it out.

Ivy moved away from him as he wiped his mouth. "Not good?" Ivy wasn't terribly good at a lot of things, but she prided herself on making coffee. And she'd done it before here on the island.

"It tastes like the ocean." He extended the cup to her. "Taste it."

"I don't want to taste it."

"You didn't have any?"

She regarded him, a flirty feeling moving through her. "That kiss already had my heart pumping a little too hard."

Surprise crossed Mason's face. "Is that right?" He set his coffee cup on the sand. "I think the waves must've washed over our coffee supply."

"It's going to be a long six days until I call Iris then," she said coolly, though she'd seen that edged, desire-filled look currently in Mason's eyes on other men's faces. She reached up and pulled her hair out of the sandy ponytail she'd slept in. Working her fingers through her hair, she managed to get some of the sand out.

"Why's that?" Mason asked, his voice a little strained.

"Because you're kind of a beast without your coffee," she said, leaning in close and touching her lips

79

to his. She wasn't sure how long ago the engagement had ended, but it didn't matter. Mason knew right where to put his hands, and exactly how to kiss her like she'd never kissed a man before.

She sighed and leaned into his chest, both of them facing the water again. "Maybe you'll have to kiss me every morning instead," he said.

"Maybe."

They sat together for several minutes, until finally Mason stood up. "Okay," he said with a sigh. "Let's get things a little more cleaned up. We can bring the furniture out to dry. Go through the food and see what else was infused with saltwater."

Ivy didn't want to do any of that, but Mason wouldn't play cards with her anymore. She wanted to spend more time with him, so she stood up and brushed the sand from her shorts. "All right, but I'm warning you. I'm not very strong."

"You can hold the door," he said with a grin.

Ivy ended up doing that while Mason pulled the furniture from the cabin. He'd brought a broom, and she swept out the interior of the building while he fed partially wet fronds and leaves to the fire.

He scrambled eggs and pulled out already cooked ham and heated it. They paused to eat, and then he said, "Anything in a plastic package or a can seems to be okay." He surveyed the food he'd put on the dining room table that had saved them from the rain and falling debris during the storm.

Ivy picked up the open bag of coffee she'd pulled from that morning. "But not this." She lifted it to her nose, and it still certainly smelled like coffee. Fine, there was a definite hint of wetness and salt.

She set it back down and looked over everything else. It seemed like such a mess, and she turned away from it. "I need to go for a walk." She strode away, only taking a couple of steps before Mason called after her.

"You want company?"

Always. Ivy always wanted someone with her. She didn't like being alone, and she wondered if she'd eventually smother Mason. "I'm okay," she said over her shoulder. She hadn't gone anywhere on the island without him since arriving.

She didn't have to go very far to get away from their camp—which was truly a camp now that they had a house with no roof. The trees obscured everything, and she felt like she was lost the moment she couldn't see Mason through the foliage. She kept the water on her right side, always in view, as she walked.

Her heart pumped, and her breathing increased, but she didn't slow down or stop. Ivy didn't mind a good workout, but she'd want a cup of hot chocolate afterward. She couldn't believe that she'd once thought that three months without hot chocolate would be the hardest part of her time on this island.

She heard the gurgle of the spring, and she turned inland to visit it. Maybe she just needed to cool down.

Get a drink that didn't come from a bottle. Soak up the sun.

She did that, putting her head under the water as it trickled off the rocks and fell into the shallow pool below. She was tired of being wet, but she lay down in the pool anyway and stared up into the blue sky.

"Iris," she said as if she could talk to her sister right now. "He's incredible, and he just kissed me." She let the happiness move through her, enjoying the emotion. "I'm not going too fast, I swear. We've been out here for nine days. Well, today is day nine, but you know what I mean."

She paused, as if her twin would have something to say.

"Anyway, the yacht is useless. We had this storm come through, and—" Ivy's voice cut out as if God himself had muted her.

The storm.

Long Bar Island was only two hours from Getaway Bay. If they'd had the storm here, would it hit the main island too? And what would the devastation be?

There had been a tropical storm a few years ago, right after the huge Sweet Breeze Resort and Hotel had gone up. Ivy knew, because everyone on the island too close to the beach had been advised to get to the hotel, floors four and above.

Ivy and Iris had shared a room in the hotel, free of charge. She'd been to a few parties there over the years as well. Sweet Breeze had amazing pools, on a half-dozen decks, and the singles life loved to hang out poolside and flirt.

Ivy had used to love that.

Now? Now, she was floating in a pool, no drink in her hand, and no one around her, vying for her attention.

"Did the storm hit the island?" she asked, almost desperate for Iris to somehow communicate with her and let her know either way. Twins had that freaky twin-thing, but Ivy wasn't getting any bizarre feelings or brain waves.

In the storm from a few years ago, the island had lost electricity for four days. No WiFi. No cell phone signals. Things had been in chaos for a while, until emergency services could get all of the essentials back in place for people.

Maybe she wouldn't be able to call Iris and explain the situation. Justin would likely be busy with his Navy SEAL friends helping residents to dry out their homes, put in new windows, and secure clean drinking water.

"It's okay, though," she told the sky, the universe, anyone and anything out there. "We have food and water. We're okay here."

And she was. Yes, she missed her family. But she was okay here. She had Mason—a very good kisser—and she had this pool to lie in when she needed a good heart-to-heart with herself.

Eventually, she pulled herself from the pool and squeezed as much water from her hair as she could. With it all secured into another tight ponytail, she found the path that would take her through the trees and back to the camp.

She wanted to ask Mason about the storm and if he thought it had hit the mainland. They needed a plan in case Iris didn't panic when Ivy didn't call on Monday. Worry bumped in her veins already, and she wasn't even expecting anyone to know they needed help for five more days.

Her shoes squelched as she walked down the narrow path, but the sun was already beginning to dry her clothes. With her stomach growling, she thought if she could just get some food inside her, she'd feel better.

Then it wouldn't matter that most of their coffee had been ruined. That they had no way to communicate with anyone. That their roof had been stolen by the wind.

She had Mason, and while he hadn't answered her question about them having a possible love connection, they definitely had one.

Possibly, she reminded herself. It was only day nine, after all.

She emerged from the trees, expecting to see Mason lying down somewhere. He'd been restless last night, and he had to be tired today. Ivy felt one breath away from pure exhaustion, but she didn't want to nap until later that afternoon.

After eating. After planning. After more kissing.

But Mason wasn't lying in the sand, napping. He wasn't sitting on the log by the fire. He wasn't going through supplies.

He was gone.

CHAPTER TEN

Mason knew very little about electronics, though he had earned a Boy Scout merit badge in electricity and electronics growing up. He wondered if Ivy would be impressed by that. No one else seemed to care that he was an Eagle Scout, something his mother had pushed him to become.

She'd said it would matter one day.

He did suppose his swimming skills and emergency preparedness skills had helped him plan for this trip—and now the aftermath of this storm.

He pulled on a blue wire, sure it was the one he needed to strip and reconnect to the underside of the radio to get it working again. If he could just get a message out, he was sure someone could come rescue them.

He wasn't sure why he was so desperate for someone to know they needed help, only that he was.

It was one thing living on this island when he had an easy way back to running water, an ATM, and civilization.

It was quite another thinking he might be stranded out here indefinitely, without someone who even knew he needed help.

Using the pocketknife he kept in the first aid kit on the bridge, he peeled back the rubber around the end of the wire. Just a little bit more....

He bit his lip, his arms starting to burn from how he held them above his head. He finally got enough wire exposed, and he touched it to the underside of the control panel, really no idea what he was doing.

Or what would happen.

So when a shower of sparks rained down on his face, his first instinct was to cover his eyes, nose, and mouth. He did, stinging starting in his fingertips and landing on the backs of his hands and arms.

That stinging became a wave of pain as he realized he'd been shocked, and burned. The back of his skull rumbled, and he kept his eyes closed, hoping the pain would subside.

With a jolt—literally—he realized his body was still in contact with the live wire, and he rolled out from underneath the controls.

But hey, there was electricity here. Too bad the Boy Scouts had never taught him how to rewire a radio on a yacht.

He lay there on the floor, breathing and taking stock

of his body. When he finally looked at his hands, his fingertips along his right hand were red, puffy, and blistering. He'd burned three of them badly—his middle finger, pointer, and thumb.

A groan started low in his throat, and he examined the slighter burns on the backs of his hands and arms. They seemed okay, though one spot wept blood. He had a first aid kit; he'd get himself doctored up.

After that...honestly, he was thinking he'd take a nap right here on the yacht. Out of the sun. He couldn't get back in the salty, ocean water with his injuries. He could yell to Ivy from the yacht, maybe even ask her to join him.

He hadn't liked her walking away from him, mostly because he could tell she was upset about something. He didn't know what. She'd been flirtatious and coy that morning on the beach, and all she'd done since was carry out a few boxes of supplies while he hauled out the heavier items.

She'd stood at the table with him. Hung up a few things to dry from her suitcase. And then walked away.

She had a bond with her family he didn't understand. He'd thought maybe that was why. But he also knew she didn't like to be alone, and she'd gone off alone.

He'd watched her until the trees had swallowed her. Then he'd finished hanging out his own wet clothes and decided to get the radio working on the yacht. He could do it. He knew he could.

He'd hotwired tractors before, and he'd dressed a cowboy's wounds with an Ace bandage and baling twine in the past. He could get this blasted radio working, because Mason was a man who did what needed to be done, no matter what supplies were available.

His next breath shuddered through his chest, but he pulled it all the way in. He couldn't afford to go into shock again, this time because of an actual injury. Crawling, he moved over to the first aid kit, which he'd abandoned on the floor several feet away, and opened it.

Band-aids, gloves, antiseptic cream. None of that would do a whole lot for burned fingertips. He could smear some of the ointment on his other wounds once they were clean, and he ended up standing up and taking the first aid kit with him down the hall to the bathroom.

Every muscle seemed clenched tight, probably from the low level of electricity that had moved through them. His throat scratched, and he took a moment to fill a glass with water so he could quench his thirst.

"There you are."

Startled, he dropped the glass, which shattered against the tile at his feet. As if he wasn't already hurt, additional pain sliced against the top of his right foot as he turned toward the female voice.

Ivy stood there, water dripping from the ends of her shorts. She had both hands cocked on her hips, and Mason could only look at her.

"What are you doing over here again?" She surveyed the situation, horror washing across those beautiful features. "Oh, holy starfish. Your foot is bleeding." She bent down and picked up the larger shards of glass. "I'm so sorry, Mason. I was just freaked out when I got back to the beach, and you were gone."

He finally got his voice to work, and he said, "I'm sorry, Ivy. I thought I'd try to get the radio working." He looked down at his hands. "But I just electrocuted myself and burned my hands."'

"You what?" Ivy straightened, alarm in her voice and evident on her face. He held up his hands so she could see.

"Starfish and octopi," she whispered. She held very still for a moment, and then she shook off the glazed look in her eyes. "It's okay. It's fine. I'll get you all fixed up." She glanced around. "Let me clean up this glass first. Neither of us needs to step on something right now."

She retreated from him, and he stayed right where he was, breathing in and out, in and out. When she returned, she had a roll of paper towels, which she proceeded to wet before sweeping the wad along the floor.

"My mother taught me this trick," she said. "You get the paper towel wet, and it picks up all the little, teeny, tiny shards of glass you can't see. You can't even sweep them up, which we can't anyway, because our broom and dustpan are on the island." She always talked more when she was nervous, but Mason didn't try to comfort her.

His hands *hurt*.

A larger shard of glass scraped against the tile, the sound offensive and grating. "I'm so sorry," Mason said again. "I feel like such a fool."

Ivy finished with the floor and tossed the mass of paper towels in the garbage can beside him. "Why?"

He couldn't look at her. "For not knowing that paper towel trick, for one. For hurting myself. And for bringing you out here." He did meet her eye then. "I'm sorry, Ivy."

Something stormed in her eyes, and it looked almost as dangerous as the tropical rains and gales they'd already survived. "I already said you couldn't control the weather, Mason."

"Did you know you were the only person who applied to come out here with me?" he asked. He shook his head. "I should've known then that this was a bad idea."

"It wasn't a bad idea," she said. "I was having a lot of fun until yesterday. Even since then." She stepped close to him and put one hand on his face. "I was really the only one who messaged you?"

He nodded, wondering what that meant. Ivy's eyelids fluttered and then drifted closed. Her breath touched his mouth, and then she kissed him. "It's fine," she whispered into his mouth. "I wanted to come, Mase."

He reached for her, recoiling when his injured flesh met her rough clothes. And they certainly weren't rough. His skin was just so tender.

"Let's get you fixed up," she said, her voice a bit higher than normal. "And then we can take a nap."

"Here?" he said. "On the yacht. Out of the sun. Out of the wind."

She swallowed and focused on the first aid kit. "Yeah, okay. Here is fine."

"You don't like the yacht?"

Ivy rummaged through the kit, pulling out various items and lining them up on the small vanity. "I feel a little trapped on a boat," she said. "Like, it could sink with me on it, and I'll never get out." She met his eye in the mirror and went back to the kit. "You know there's a submarine in Pearl Harbor full of people, right? Sunk. They're still down there."

"The USS Arizona," Mason said, his heart enlarging for this good woman. "I know about it."

"Yeah, well, boats kind of freak me out." She flashed him a smile and ripped open an antiseptic wipe. "I'm going to go all over your hands and arms with this." She met his eye. "Okay?"

"This isn't a submarine," he said, hoping to prolong the moment before she made him hurt again. "It's a yacht."

"Technicality," she said with a smile.

"You can stay in my chamber with me," he said. "If you want. No funny business."

"Good," she said, her voice light and airy again. "Because there's nothing funny going on here." She looked down at his hands and swiped the cold cloth across his skin. Instant searing hit him, and he couldn't contain the groan.

"Sorry," she said. "Sorry, sorry, sorry." She finished cleaning him up and tossed the wipe in the trashcan. "I don't think these cuts need any bandages. And the only thing I know to do about those fingers is painkiller." She shook several tablets into her hand, got a new glass of water for him, and watched him swallow them.

"Nap time?" he asked, his eyes dry and gritty.

"Yes," she said, linking her hand through his. "Oh, wait. Your foot." She made quick work of cleaning that up, bandaging it, and leading him down the steps to the cabins.

There were three with king-sized beds, and he didn't care which one they slept in. She chose the one closest to the exit, saying, "I feel like I can get out from here if the boat starts to sink."

"Yacht," he corrected, just because he could. He got in bed, glad when she did too, and a long sigh escaped from his mouth.

"I wish we had an alarm," Ivy said from the other side of the bed. He couldn't feel her body heat, which meant she'd kept way over on her side of the bed. It did feel quite intimate to be in a bed with her, though they'd been much closer physically on the sand that morning.

"Do you think you'll be able to sleep?" he asked.

"I sure hope so," she said. "I'm tired."

"Me too." he closed his eyes, the relief in them instant. "We'll be okay, Ivy." His voice dropped to a whisper. "Okay? We'll be okay."

Her hand found his beneath the covers and squeezed.

And finally, Mason slept peacefully.

CHAPTER ELEVEN

*I*vy marked each day on a little pad of paper she'd found in the drawer beside the bed where she and Mason had taken to spending their nights. When she woke in the morning, she made another mark, smiled at the still-sleeping form of Mason, and went to the island to make coffee and scramble eggs.

The routine was so common now, it felt like she'd been doing it for years instead of only seven days.

Seven days.

They only went to the yacht to sleep, something about being contained inside a room, with a roof, that made them both more comfortable than sleeping out under the stars.

"Which is weird for me, honestly," he'd told her. "I've spent my whole life out on a ranch. Many nights underneath only the stars."

Ivy had told him things were different now, and maybe he wasn't as cowboy as he thought he was. He'd pretended to be offended, and then he'd kissed her for so long that their soup had burnt to the bottom of the pot.

Eggs for breakfast. Canned soup for lunch. Protein bars in the afternoon. Oatmeal for dinner, sometimes with a swirl of syrup. At least Mason had considered bringing something sweet to abate all the bland food they were consuming.

Mason slept later than her every morning, which also seemed to be the opposite of what a cowboy would do. He hadn't explained that one yet, probably because Ivy hadn't asked.

He waded ashore, and she grinned at him from her crouched position over the fire. His foot had healed quickly, as had the small burns on his hands and arms. His fingers had been terrible, swelling and blistering and filling with liquid before he'd finally pierced them and drained the infection out.

They were still very sore, and he held his right hand above his head when he waded through the ocean from the yacht to their camp on shore.

"Morning," she said. "Day eight." She couldn't help telling him, though he knew. He'd seen her pad with the tally marks. They'd talked about a contingency plan if no one showed up to save them.

They'd stay the course. They had enough food if they were careful. There was a pool of water, and they had bottled water too. They'd simply stay for the three months they'd planned on. Surely the island would be put back together from any storms by then. And her family would for sure know something was wrong and send help.

"Day eight," Mason echoed back to her. She pulled the pan from the fire and divided the eggs in half.

"This is the last of the eggs," she said, passing him the plate.

"I know," he said. "We'll have to start eating the fruit and oatmeal bars."

He'd brought a cooler made of the finest materials, said to keep anything cold for ten days, even in the sun. The cooler he'd brought still had ice in it, but they'd eaten almost all of the perishable items already. The lunchmeat, cheese, eggs, and fruit cups. The last item could technically still be eaten, whether cold or not.

They still had a gallon of milk, and she was planning on eating cold cereal for a few days before succumbing to the oatmeal bars.

"And there are a few fruit trees here," he said.

Ivy only nodded as she scooped up a forkful of eggs. She'd heard horrible stories from Iris about the amount of fruit she'd consumed on her deserted island. She hadn't eaten fruit for many months after returning to Getaway Bay, and Ivy couldn't say she blamed her. Especially not now.

"Do you want to make a water run this morning?" he asked.

"Yeah, sure. I need to do some wash, and we can refill the bottles."

He nodded, and the silence between them settled comfortably. He didn't talk much, but Ivy had learned she didn't need him to. They'd been out on the island for sixteen full days now, and that was akin to dating a man for several months for Ivy.

And she still liked Mason a whole lot. There hadn't been any funny business in the cabin where they slept, unless she counted listening to him talk in his sleep. He also teased her about some nightmare she could never remember.

"Do you want a dog?" she asked, just to have something to talk about. She'd always wanted a day or two to just lie on the beach, but now that she'd had many, many of those, she realized she did like being busy.

"I've had several dogs over the years," he said.

"Do you own a dog right now?"

"Nope." He finished his breakfast and stretched his legs out in front of him. "My last two dogs were Smoky and Georgia. I left them on the ranch in Texas. They survived the tornado."

"Whoa, what? Tornado?"

"Yeah," he said, chuckling. "Haven't I told you this?" He rubbed his hands down his face, stroking his beard. He was quite sexy with the facial hair, and Ivy really liked it.

"No, sirree," she said in her best cowgirl twang. "I've heard nothing about a tornado. Wait. You did say you get them in the panhandle of Texas. I guess I just didn't realize you'd been in one so recently."

"Oh, I wasn't," he said. "I put the ranch up for sale, but I didn't wait for it to sell before I moved to Getaway Bay." He exhaled as he leaned back, his eyes closed and his face toward the sky. He was absolutely beautiful when relaxed as he was, and Ivy's cells warmed.

"Anyway, the ranch sold, and literally a few days after closing, there was a big tornado in Three Rivers. I heard it caused quite a bit of damage. But a neighbor down the road had the dogs, and everyone survived."

"Wow," Ivy said. "And the new ranch owners didn't get upset?"

"I haven't heard from them," he said. "A bunch of brothers bought the place. I wasn't there. I never met them."

A squirrel of unrest moved through her. "I don't own my own house." The words tasted bitter coming out of her mouth, but he should probably know.

"No? Where do you live on the island?"

"I'm close to downtown," she said. "I have a little cottage almost on the beach. I used to share with my twin, until she got married." That instant sadness hit her again, but she pushed it away. Doing so had become easier and easier the longer she went without talking to Iris, and she supposed she should be happy about that.

She stacked her plate on top of Mason's and lay down beside him.

"In the Twin Palms?"

"Yeah," she said, twisting to look at him. "You know it?"

"My real estate agent took me there when I first came to the island. But I bought a place in the new apartment buildings a little further east."

"Yeah," she said. "The ritzy places, for rich people. Did you know they have a *concierge* there?"

Mason burst out laughing, his hand slipping into hers. "Ivy," he said once he'd sobered. "I sure do like you."

"I like you too, Mason."

"This isn't terrible, is it?"

"It's…a little different than I was expecting."

He chuckled. "Yeah, me too."

They fell into silence after that, and eventually Ivy cleaned up their breakfast dishes and started packing empty bottles into her backpack. In an empty supply box, she loaded her clothes. At least they had something to do today, so they wouldn't just sit around and watch the waves.

They'd done plenty of that yesterday, when they'd expected a SEAL submarine to show up, sirens blaring.

Doing laundry and refilling water bottles at the spring took them to lunchtime. Mason made grilled cheese sandwiches with the last of their bread and cheese, and Ivy wasted some time in the afternoon by walking along the beach, her hand secured in Mason's.

Late afternoon did find them sitting on the log, watching the water for a ship Ivy knew wouldn't be coming that day.

"Ready?" Mason asked as the sky turned red and orange and gold, the sun setting behind the island.

"Yeah." She sighed as she got up, and Mason took her into his arms. She tried to suck back the tears, but her chest shook with the effort. "I'm okay," she said, though her voice was much too high and gave away all of her emotions.

"I know you are," he said. "Ivy, you're incredible. Just amazing. I'm sorry the ship didn't come today."

"Maybe tomorrow," she said, and he nodded. He took her face in his hands and looked at her, those dark eyes full of so much adoration. More than she'd ever seen, even in the eyes of Brooks, who she'd thought would ask her to marry him.

Of course, she'd been dead wrong about that. She could be dead wrong about this too.

"Maybe tomorrow," Mason echoed, and then he held her hand with his left one, keeping his right out of the saltwater, and guided them back to the yacht for another night's rest.

IVY WOKE IN THE MIDDLE OF THE NIGHT, THE spot where Mason slept next to her empty and cold. He was gone again.

Her adrenaline spiked, and she sat up suddenly. Pure darkness covered everything in the cabin, and she scrambled to switch on the lamp on the bedside table. Maybe he'd just gone to get a drink. Gone to the bathroom. Make a midnight bowl of oatmeal—though why he'd do that eluded her.

She didn't find him in the bathroom or the kitchen, and she paused on the threshold of stepping out of the areas down-below and going out into the open air of the night. It wasn't cold, but a shiver worked its way through her anyway, and she rubbed her hands up and down her arms.

She wore her pajamas—a pair of cotton shorts with a tank top—which didn't seem adequate to be roaming around a yacht. A noise above her cause a yelp to come out of her mouth, and she backed into the dining room table, the backs of her knees hitting the bench and making her fall into a sitting position.

Sucking in a breath, she managed to contain the scream. A moment later, Mason appeared.

"Where have you been?" she asked, her heart hammering out of control.

He flinched and froze, alarm crossing his face too. He searched the darkness for her, his eyes finally meeting hers. "The bridge."

"You're still working on that radio?" She stood up

and crossed the space between them. After examining his hands, she looked into those eyes she liked so much. "No wonder you sleep so late. How long have you been up?"

"Hours," he admitted. "I usually slip away as soon as I know you're asleep."

"So I'm down there by myself?" She cast a long look over her shoulder, as if there would be a demon hovering there, ready to drag her down to a watery grave.

Mason just nodded. "I can't get it to work, though there's electricity coming in."

"I told you, someone will come."

"What if they don't, Ivy?" he challenged. "Then what?"

"Then we row north," she barked.

Mason shook his head. "I don't want to argue. I'm tired." He stepped past her as if he'd leave her standing there on the cusp of being exposed, alone. She hurried after him, her anger growing with each silent second between them.

"Mason," she said once they'd entered the cabin. "I don't think you should waste your time and energy with that radio."

He pulled his T-shirt over his head and got in bed, turning away from her. "I can't just give up."

"It's not giving up."

"I don't quit."

"It's not quitting." She sat on her side of the bed,

her back to him too. "It's called being smart. Spending time and resources on the right things."

"And what are those, Ivy? In case you haven't noticed, we're not busy out here. Who cares if I spend a few hours working on the radio?"

"Why couldn't you tell me about it then?"

"Because I knew you'd react this way." He sounded so tired, and Ivy didn't want to argue with him either.

"I don't want to be down here by myself."

"Fair enough," he said. "I apologize for that."

She lay down and turned toward him, slipping her hand onto his shoulder. "We're going to be fine, Mason."

"I know that, Ivy."

Still, she felt like he had more to say. When he didn't vocalize it, she took a chance. "What aren't you telling me?"

Another lengthy silence followed. So long, Ivy thought Mason had fallen asleep. Finally, he said. "I'm not sure I'm cut out to live in Hawaii, Ivy."

CHAPTER TWELVE

*M*ason listened to Ivy suck in a breath.

"But I live in Hawaii," she said.

Yes, she did. And he didn't know what to say to her. He'd known he wasn't supposed to be in Texas. But was he supposed to be here?

"I felt so good about this island adventure," he said, his voice sounding loud in the silence. "And it's been a complete disaster."

"Complete?" she asked, her hand slipping away from his shoulder.

"We're stuck out here," he whispered. "No one's coming."

"We've talked about this," she said. "We're two hours from the mainland. We have food."

"We're two hours by yacht," he said. "With a motor. I can't row us back there in one hundred and twenty minutes." He didn't mean to sound so angry. He wasn't mad at her. Only himself.

"I don't know what I'm doing with my life," he whispered, his eyes open but unseeing. It was so dark on the yacht. So dark out here in the middle of the ocean.

"Do you want another ranch?" she asked. "I think there's a macadamia nut farm for sale. You could do that. I'm great with keeping books."

She was thinking long-term with him, and Mason smiled. "I don't know, Ivy. I feel lost, out here on this island. And not just physically. I…." He didn't want to admit anything to her, but if not her, then who?

The little old lady who lived next door and walked her two white dogs three times a day just to have something to do? Drake Summers, who worked on the cattle ranch and just wanted Mason's extra set of hands?

"I thought if I came out here, I could figure things out."

A blip of silence passed. Then Ivy asked, "Why did you advertise to find a girlfriend then?"

"I didn't want to be alone."

Ivy's hand touched his, and he lifted his arm so she could slide into his side. She did, and a sense of relief pulled through him. "See? I'm not the only one who doesn't like to be alone."

He chuckled, the sound so foreign among all the

darkness. "I think if we ever come to this island again, we should only plan to stay for the day."

"Did you ever sleep on it when you were building the cabin?"

"No," he said. "It kinda scared me."

"You?" she teased. "You're a rough, tough, muscley cowboy."

"Muscley?"

"Well, you have big muscles." She giggled into his side, sobering quickly. "You're not really going to leave Getaway Bay, are you?"

"I doubt it," he said. "I just want to get off this island so badly. I don't want you to...be upset with me."

"I'm not upset with you." She'd reassured him of similar things several times since the storm, but Mason felt like one giant failure.

He pressed his lips to the top of her head and closed his eyes. In his mind, he could see the wires underneath the console on the bridge. If he could just find the right ones....

When he woke, he was alone, and he wondered how that was fair. Ivy didn't like being alone when she woke up, but she left him snoozing on the yacht every morning. She claimed to have developed an early-rising habit when she became a gym rat, going to workout every morning at five-thirty, rain or shine.

He'd asked her if it ever really rained in Hawaii, and

she'd laughed. "Lots of rain," she said. "We're tropical."

And of course, now that he'd lived through a tropical storm, he definitely knew it rained—a lot.

He got up and got dressed, made the bed, and waded ashore. Ivy wasn't near the fire, though it smoked, so she'd definitely been there. "Ivy?" he called, glancing down the beach. She didn't come out from the trees, and he moved to pick up a water bottle, only a blip of concern running through him.

There were no animals on the island. Nowhere to go. Wherever she'd gone and whatever she was doing, she'd be back. "But she hates to go out to the spring alone," he mused. The only thing Ivy did alone was go to the bathroom. And change her clothes. Other than that, she stayed by Mason's side, or he stuck by hers.

They did everything together, and Mason had once thought he wouldn't like that. Anne-Marie had nearly smothered him, but Ivy was so unlike her. She didn't try to change Mason. Make him wear shirts that scratched just so he'd look "more polished."

Anne-Marie had often bought his boots so he'd stand out. She tried to get him to look and play a part, and while he'd been miserable when she'd given back the ugly ring he'd bought her, he didn't *miss* her.

He thought he'd miss Ivy.

"Mason," she said, the word an explosion of breath from her mouth. He spun toward her to find her stumbling under the weight of several palm fronds. She was panting, and she dropped the load she carried as soon as their eyes met.

"Go put the flag up. There's a ship."

"Really?" His heart boomed in his chest, huge gonging sounds that sent reverberations through his muscles. "Where?"

"It went around that side," she said, pointing to the cliffs. "It can't see us. We need to make smoke and get them to come back."

"What if—?"

"If you put up the flag, maybe they'll see it above the cliffs." She sucked at the air as she bent down. "Hurry."

He didn't think raising the flag on the yacht would help at all. And the mechanism to do it was powered by electricity, and who knew if that would work? It didn't work for the radio.

"The smoke should get them back," he said, looking into the trees. "Should I run to the other side of the island? Maybe I'll see them over there."

"I don't know," Ivy said, blowing on the fire. Her voice bordered on hysterical. "We have to get them to come back. I can't believe they didn't see me or the island."

"How far away were they?" he asked, taking a couple of steps to her and touching her shoulder. "Calm down. Take it easy. You're going to inhale that smoke and fall head-first into the fire."

She looked at him, a wildness in her eyes. Scraping

her hair out of her face, she breathed. "They were still quite a ways out."

"Did it look like a rescue ship?"

"I couldn't tell."

So maybe it wasn't. Could be someone out yachting for the day. *Which doesn't matter*, he told himself. If he could get them to come to the island, he and Ivy could get back to civilization.

"I'm going to go to the other side of the island," he said, making a quick decision. "You're okay here by yourself?"

"Yes." She nodded, though she looked like she might cry. "Yes, I'll be fine."

Mason took a moment to kiss her fiercely, and then he jogged into the trees. His mind sprinted faster than his legs, but he was able to seize onto one thought—*get a frond*. If he could do that, then he could wave it, making himself bigger, brighter.

The island had never seemed that big to him before —until he was trying to run across it before a rescue vessel left sight of the island. He wasn't sure how long he ran, only that his legs and lungs ached and he was covered in sweat by the time he saw water in front of him.

Relief propelled him to take a few more strides, and then a few more. He broke through the trees, and there, on the horizon, sat a ship.

"Hey!" he yelled, waving his arms above his head. The ship was definitely a yacht, not a rescue boat, but he hardly cared. They needed help, and he would take it in any form that had a motor.

Frantic now, he stepped over to the nearest palm tree and ripped off the biggest branch he could. He waved it back and forth, his biceps screaming at him to stop. With all the running and now the waving, they weren't terribly happy.

He didn't care. He walked awkwardly down the beach, waving and yelling, until his feet hit the water. And still he kept going. Maybe he and Ivy should've stomped out the word HELP in the sand. Or had a fire on both sides of the island. He hadn't even thought of doing so, because the side where he'd built the cabin and they'd been camping faced north—faced Getaway Bay.

"Hey!" he yelled. "Come back!"

The yacht moved mostly away from him, and unless someone came around to the stern of the ship, they wouldn't see him. And he knew better than most that it wasn't silent on a boat. Even the waves coming ashore were noisy.

Movement on the boat caught his eye, and he gave everything he had to his voice, yelling again so loudly that it hurt his throat.

Whoever had come around the back of the ship lifted their head. The yacht was easily a few hundred yards away, maybe more, but he waved his palm frond with everything he had.

"We need help! Help!"

The figure pointed, waved both arms above their head, and disappeared.

Mason dropped the palm frond and fell to his knees, his chest heaving. He wished he had a phone so he could call Ivy and tell her to come to the other side of the island. But he didn't, and he could barely breathe. He may have muscles, but he was not a runner.

He turned back toward the beach—and froze.

Thick, white smoke filled the air above the trees, a much bigger signal than the one he'd given. A smile filled his face, and he started laughing.

"Way to go, Ivy," he said to the sky. "You did it."

CHAPTER THIRTEEN

*O*nce Mason had gone, Ivy let the tears roll down her face. She worked through the blurry vision, having had a great amount of experience of crying while still getting things done. She'd fill the whole sky with smoke. So much that people sunbathing on the beach in the East Bay would see it and wonder what was happening.

She would.

The greenery smoked well, and she tended to it to make sure she didn't smother out the flame. She eventually stopped crying, but she had no way of knowing if the ship was even facing their island. It could be a crew of one, someone just out for a fun day on the water.

Of course, if that were true, why hadn't Iris sent help? Why hadn't Eden?

Ivy should've checked in two days ago, and she and Mason had come to the conclusion that the storm that had knocked them around had done the same to Getaway Bay. Perhaps the harbors and docks were shut down, something that happened after a big storm. The rescue boats wanted to be able to get around easily, and it was harder with vacationers or islanders out on their boats.

An astronomical amount of time seemed to pass, and Mason didn't return. Neither did the ship. Ivy didn't know what to do, so she darted back into the trees to get more palm fronds. She would keep this smoke signal going until she knew for certain she didn't need to.

Her stomach roared with the want of food, because she'd only opened a box of blueberry oatmeal bars before she'd caught sight of the ship. She hadn't actually taken a bite, and she had no idea where the bar had gone.

She'd yelled for Mason, who hadn't heard her, of course.

She'd waded out into the water as far as she dared, waving and yelling. The ship had sailed on.

And then she'd decided to build the fire and get as much smoke into the air as she could.

A strange sound filled the air, and Ivy straightened, looking around her. It was definitely a machine. A motor. Something growing louder and getting closer. Could the ship be coming back?

Her heart pounding through every vein, she

dropped her fronds and ran for the beach. It wasn't a ship making that noise.

"A helicopter." Ivy's breath left her body even as everything inside her started to rejoice. She tipped her head up as the helicopter approached, laughter spilling from her throat. Waving her arms, she caught sight of Justin in the co-pilot's chair, his face stoic.

So like him.

She didn't care. He'd come. Iris had sent help.

"Mason." Ivy whipped back toward the forest behind her, wondering where Mason was and how quickly he could make it back to the beach. On a helicopter, they could be back to a hot shower in an hour. If that.

And then they could make arrangements to come back and clean up. Get the yacht fixed. Get it towed. Whatever. Mason had a ton of money, and he'd take care of all of it.

Just like he'd taken care of her. Tried to fix the radio in the middle of the night so she wouldn't be worried. Yes, she'd helped him too, and she thought they made a pretty great team.

The helicopter circled the island, finally coming back toward her. She ducked into the cabin as sand started spraying everywhere, the noise louder than she knew sound could be. She ducked into the corner, both hands over her ears, until the noise subsided a little bit.

"Ivy," Justin called, and she darted out the front door and into his arms.

"You came. Thank all the starfish in the sea that you came."

He held her right against him. "We got hit with a category four hurricane a few days ago. Looks like you guys took it too."

"Yeah." She stepped back and looked up into his chiseled face. "Iris sent you?"

"I've radioed her already," he said with a smile. "But yeah. She said you would've checked in, no matter what. Wouldn't leave me alone." He grinned fully then, and it was clear he loved his wife. "And good call on that smoke. Your location came through loud and clear."

Pride filled Ivy. She had done a good thing with the smoke signal. "So you brought a helicopter."

He shrugged and turned back to the chopper. "I mean, I know people." He waved at the man still in the cockpit, and once the blades fully stopped, he climbed down. "You remember Heath Hawkins? He's available if this little love tryst doesn't work out." He lifted his eyebrows, all the questions right there in those eyes.

But Ivy didn't want to talk to him about what had happened on the island. So she shrugged. "I mean, I don't know."

"You didn't like Mason?"

"I mean, we get along okay," she said, flashing Justin a look that said *drop it* as Heath approached. She hadn't lied. She and Mason got along okay. And really well. And she liked him more than she'd thought she would.

But she tended to fall too fast, and maybe she wanted to hold on a little longer before any decisions were made.

"Ivy," Mason said, and she turned toward the wonderful sound of his voice.

She hurried toward him, joy spiraling through her and making her grin at him. "There you are. My sister sent a *helicopter*."

"The yacht is coming around too," he said, taking her into his arms when she threw herself at him. He held her tight, and it was so different than when Justin did it. "We get along just okay?" he whispered into her hair.

Ivy jerked away, her pulse ricocheting around inside her chest. She really needed to take it easy on all the adrenaline spikes. She might end up in cardiac arrest.

"I only said that—"

A loud horn covered her words and drew her attention to the water in front of her.

"There's the yacht," Mason said, walking toward the water.

"What should we take back now?" Justin asked.

"I can help get it hooked up," Heath said to Mason, who shook his hand. "Did you ask them to tow it back?"

"I was thinking we'd go with them," Mason said. "I flagged them down before you guys showed up." He kept talking, but they'd moved far enough away from Ivy that she couldn't hear him anymore.

Her heart pinched against her ribs, and she wished she could reach inside her chest and adjust it.

It's fine, she told herself. She could talk to Mason later. Explain everything. If there was one thing she was good at, it was talking.

"Ivy," Justin said, extending his phone toward her. "It's Iris."

Emotion swelled and swirled, and Ivy teared up as she took Justin's phone from him and said, "Hey, Iris."

"Oh, my word, it's her. It's her, everyone. Are you okay, Ivy? Talk to me. Tell me what happened."

But for once, Ivy couldn't talk. She watched Mason and Heath hoist themselves up onto the other yacht and talk to the man standing at the stern.

"You fell in love with him, didn't you?" Iris demanded. "I'm going to assume yes unless you say something."

"We got hit by a tropical storm," Ivy said, swallowing her emotions. "Our phones were soaking wet. Radio shorted out. The wind took off the roof." It wasn't exactly a no, but it wasn't a yes either.

Mason was a complicated man, though he seemed simple on the surface. And Ivy was simple when she seemed complicated. Could they have a future together?

Iris's voice registered in her ear again, and as much as Ivy wanted to tell her everything right that moment, she couldn't. "Iris," she said. "I'm okay. Mason is okay. Things are fine. I'm not going to pass out like you did."

"Yeah, you guys had food," Iris said.

"How's everything on the island?" she asked.

"Um, well, the storm that hit Long Bar Island swirled out in the ocean for days and days, picking up strength and speed," she said.

Ivy waited, because in this case, strength and speed weren't good.

"And you can stay with me and Justin until we find you a new place to live."

"My house is gone?" Ivy's voice pitched up way too high. Justin turned back toward her, alarm on his face.

"It's a teensy bit…gone," Iris said. "That beachside community was totally wiped out. Thankfully, everyone evacuated."

"Did you get anything from my house?" She thought of the super-bionic blender she'd spent a month's earnings on during her smoothie stage. She loved that blender.

"Sorry, sis," Iris said. "When the storm turned, it *turned*. Everyone was scrambling for higher ground."

Ivy sighed, though she knew exactly what it was like to live through a hurricane. The days leading up to it, the terrifying time riding it out, the aftermath. The clean-up.

"Thank you for sending Justin," she said. "It couldn't have been easy to get authorization."

"I sat outside the Navy commander's office for eighteen hours," Iris said. "Justin was so embarrassed."

For some reason, that made Ivy laugh, and then Iris did too, and suddenly everything was okay.

"See you soon," she said, and they hung up. She handed the phone back to Justin and asked, "How much can I bring?"

"How much do you have?"

She shaded her eyes as she looked out to the yacht. Mason was on his now, working with a chain while Heath and the other owner stayed on-board the working vessel.

"Maybe we can load everything onto the yacht," she said. "And I'll just fly back with you."

"You're the boss, Ivy," Justin said. "Put me to work."

"Let's ask Mason." She waded into the water. "Mase," she called. "Should I have him start to bring stuff back to the yacht? We can ride back in the helicopter."

He paused in his work and looked down at her from the deck. "Sure, let's get everything on board the yacht," he said. "But I'll go with Joe on his yacht. You can fly back with Justin if you want."

She nodded and then looked at Justin. "You heard him. Everything on the yacht."

Justin looked around. "You don't have a boat?"

"Smashed and then gone in the storm," Ivy said. "We'll have to go out with one thing at a time." She returned to shore, already exhausted, and this day had a lot more hours in it, with so much more to do.

But she could do it.

She'd built a fire. She'd kept Mason from starving after the storm. She'd broadcasted their position with smoke.

She could certainly haul supplies from the beach to the yacht.

And then she'd get back to civilization, take a hot shower, and tell her family that they'd been right. She shouldn't have thought she could survive for three months out on a deserted island.

Or that she could fall in love with the surly cowboy who'd proposed the idea in the first place.

But maybe you could have, her mind whispered. *And maybe you did.*

Warmth filled Ivy, iced when Mason looked at her, his eyes cold. "See you on the island," he said as the last box was placed on board by Justin. They both jumped back into the water, and Justin came toward her while Mason climbed aboard the other yacht.

He didn't look back as they started out slowly, *Starlight* groaning as she finally moved away from the cliffs where she'd been stuck for over a week.

CHAPTER FOURTEEN

*W*e get along okay.

Ivy's words wouldn't stop stinging Mason's mind.

He thought they got along better than okay. She kissed him like she liked him better than okay.

I only said that—

Those four words kept cropping up in his mind too. Maybe she just hadn't wanted to reveal how she felt about him to her brother-in-law. Maybe she wasn't really sure. Heaven knew Mason wasn't really sure.

But Mason wasn't really sure about anything right now. He knew he wanted to get back to the mainland. Anchor his yacht at the dock and deal with it later.

Go home.

Take a shower.

Find a dog to live with.

One thing he'd learned about himself out on the

island was how much he liked talking to someone else. He wondered if the person—or animal—mattered, or if he just liked talking to Ivy. He had his suspicions, and he found himself wishing she were with him instead of on the helicopter.

Then he could ask her if he'd become chattier as they grew to know each other better. He could find out what she meant by *we get along okay*. He could stop wondering if he'd made a huge mistake by leaving Texas and coming to Getaway Bay.

The yacht cruised along, pulling his broken-down vessel behind them. He was grateful for Jacob Spendlove, who hadn't hesitated when Mason had explained the situation. He said he had chains, and he could get them all back to Getaway Bay.

For the twenty minutes it had taken to go back around to the other side of the island, Mason had thought he'd be a hero. Then he'd heard the helicopter blades, and those hopes had faded.

"They were stupid anyway," he muttered to himself. Ivy didn't need him to be a hero. She could take care of herself.

"Are you hungry?" Jacob asked, his British accent jarring Mason out of his own thoughts.

"No, I'm okay," Mason said, though his stomach did complain loudly for food. He glanced down at his shirt as they both started chuckling. "I guess I could eat."

"My wife has coffee ready," he said. "And flapjacks."

Mason ate with Jacob and Madeliene, and they

talked about whales and the ocean and the storm that had hit the island a few days ago.

"Tell me more about that," Mason said.

"Oh, it was terrible," Jacob said. "We don't have hurricanes in England."

Madeliene said, "We had to move into the hotel. Our bed and breakfast was too close to the shoreline. And it's a good thing we did." She shook her fork at Mason as if lecturing him. "The water went up eight inches. You could see the marks on the walls."

"Wow," Mason said, glad he'd bought an apartment on the tenth floor. Suddenly, the thought of returning to that apartment filled him with dread. He'd be alone again, and while he'd once craved isolation, he found now that he didn't like it.

The helicopter would arrive back in Getaway Bay hours before the limping yachts, and he kept one ear on the conversation at the breakfast table while thinking about Ivy. They hadn't exactly separated on good terms, though he supposed he couldn't just kiss her openly in front of everyone.

Why not? his mind whispered. *If she's your girlfriend, why not?*

The truth, he didn't know what Ivy was. Extraordinary circumstances had brought them together. They were supposed to have three months to figure things out. They'd had less than a week before the storm hit, and then things had been different. He'd been different. He'd changed as he tried to fix the radio in the wee hours of the night, as they both counted down days and then hours. As disappointments became realities.

The yacht did eventually make it back to the dock, and Jacob helped Mason secured his rig. Then he took the only bag he'd brought aboard and said, "Thank you so much for everything. Really, you're lovely people."

"Do you have a ride?" Jacob asked, looking around the parking lot.

"I suppose not." Mason had planned on calling Henley when he was ready to go back to the apartment. He would've brought the car, and Mason hadn't given it a second thought. Until now.

Ivy's car was somewhere too. She'd probably gone home with a family member, and he certainly didn't have a phone he could call or text her with.

"We'll drop you," Madeliene said. "Let's go."

FORTY-FIVES MINUTES LATER, MASON SIGHED as he pressed his back against the now closed and locked door of his apartment. He didn't have keys to his building or his house, and a manager had to be called.

Henley hadn't asked any questions, but they all swam in his eyes. Mason had finally gotten away from everyone once he'd cleared the security questions and been allowed to come up to his apartment with the manager.

She'd said she'd get him some new keys by tomorrow, and he didn't plan on leaving the apartment until then. He didn't have much food, but he could order it. He could send Henley. Whatever it took to just stay behind blinded windows and out of the wind, sun, and elements.

The island was a bit of a mess, as everyone was still cleaning up from the storm. If Ivy hadn't been related to a Navy SEAL, Mason felt certain the two of them would still be stranded out on Long Bar Island.

He showered, the hot water more delightful than he thought possible. He'd always prided himself on being a rough and tumble cowboy. He could eat anything. Sleep anywhere. Go days without showering or shaving.

But he didn't *have* to, and he was starting to realize he liked the more civilized parts of life too.

He stood at the windows as the sun went down, his partial reflection in front of him. "What do you want?" he asked himself.

And the biggest problem was—he had no idea.

Sighing, he turned away from the windows and the glorious view and flipped open his laptop. It took several seconds to start up, and then dozens and dozens of chimes filled the air.

"Holy starfish," he said, very aware he'd just used

Ivy's expletive. He turned down the volume as the notifications kept coming and coming and coming.

"What is going on?" He clicked and read, trying to figure out where all the noises were coming from. When he did, he sat down heavily in the chair in front of the desk.

There were well over two hundred messages in his chatbox now, the one he'd set up to use for the ad. He hadn't gotten any of them before, but they were definitely there now. He leaned forward, looking for the timestamps. Many, many of them came in before Ivy's had.

How had he not seen these?

"Maybe the idea wasn't crazy," he said to the empty apartment. But the way his heart felt full of ashes testified that it definitely was. After all, what had he achieved?

"Nothing." He closed the laptop, the sharp click of it so satisfying. He really felt like he hadn't accomplished much—except maybe losing his heart to a pretty blonde woman who used octopi as a way to express her awe.

A DAY PASSED, AND THEN TWO. HE GOT NEW keys for his apartment. Henley got his car out of storage. He bought his own groceries, picked up a new cell phone, and called someone about fixing the yacht.

With everything going on in his personal life and around the island, he didn't worry too much that he hadn't seen Ivy. She needed time to do all of those things too, and there were still some parts of the island in complete disarray.

Whole communities had been washed away. The small cottages on the beach had been hit particularly hard, and Mason decided to go down to one and volunteer. Tons of debris needed to be hauled away, and the rebuilding had already begun for some people lucky enough to have family and friends to help.

Mason wondered what he would do if his house was wiped off the face of the Earth. He had no family here, and in fact, no one in his family had even known about the storm and where he'd been.

He hadn't spent a lot of time exploring the island, but when he turned where a volunteer told him to, he saw three signs someone had leaned up against a tree trunk. All of the branches had lost their fronds, and the tree reminded him of a skeleton.

Sandy Shores.

Tropical Paradise.

Twin Palms.

"Twin Palms," he said, his heartbeat accelerating. He parked and got out, glancing around for where the Twin Palms beach cottages were. He'd looked here when he'd first moved to the island.

Ivy lived here.

He hurried over to the blue tent that had been set

up for volunteers. "Do you need help in Twin Palms today?" he asked.

"Uh, let me see," the woman behind the table said. "Twin Palms is almost cleared." She shook her head. "They're only pulling the bigger things out now. Going to turn it into a beach dog park."

"What?" he asked. "What about the homes?"

"Everything was destroyed in Twin Palms," she said, looking at him oddly. "You didn't know?"

He wanted to bark at her, ask her why he should know that. Instead, he spun away from the volunteer booth, almost desperate to find Ivy now. Of course, she wasn't standing there. Turning back to the woman, he asked, "Do you know where the residents went?"

"Most are staying with family or at the Sweet Breeze Resort," she said. "They put up anyone who didn't have a home."

Ivy had plenty of family on the island. Mason just needed to find them.

"Do you happen to know the McLaughlin's?" he asked.

The woman's face lit up. "Sure. The girls who all got stranded and fell in love?" She sighed. "Makes you want to get on a boat and just hope something happens, right?" She giggled like being stranded on an island would be a picnic.

Mason had thought that too, once.

He forced a laugh out of his mouth. "Right. So...do you know them?"

"Sure, I mean, I know *of* them." She pointed to something on someone's clipboard, her attention diverted for a moment.

"Where could I find them?" Mason asked, trying to school his voice into being kind. He sort of succeeded.

"Well, the one, she married the owner of Explore Getaway Bay. And another one...I don't know what happened to her. But another is marrying the quarter-back of the Orcas in a few months. Her name is Orchid. I remember, because Orchid sounds a lot like Orcas." The woman beamed at him, and Mason smiled right on back.

"Thank you," he said, tipping his cowboy hat and making a beeline for his car. Orchid McLaughlin. Not married yet.

She shouldn't be too hard to find, not for someone like Mason, with unlimited resources and time.

And if he couldn't do it, he'd ask Henley to help him. That man could find a pinhead in the sand.

CHAPTER FIFTEEN

"You're not going to work again?" Orchid paused by the front door when she realized Ivy was still on the couch, in her pajamas.

"No," Ivy said, not much more of an explanation in her. Orchid had been so amazing to let her bunk with Tesla, and Ivy had been helping out with her niece in the afternoons before Orchid got off work.

She'd given up her job at the boutique, and with everything that had happened since she'd returned to Getaway Bay, she couldn't face going back there and trying to get her position back.

Not yet, anyway.

"Are you okay?" Orchid asked, coming closer and leaning over the way their mother had done when the girls were sick. She stroked Ivy's hair off her forehead and tucked it behind her ear.

"Fine." Ivy smiled up at her. "Now go on. You'll be late. I'll get Tesla and have dinner on the table when you get home."

"Maine's taking us to dinner tonight," Orchid said. "End-of-year banquet for the Orcas. You don't need to cook."

"Okay." Ivy sat up as her sister walked back to the door. She waved at Tesla and Orchid as they left, and then she frowned at the closed door. The silence.

She'd gotten a new phone the day after returning on the helicopter. She'd been staying with Orchid ever since, because her cottage was literally a pile of sticks spread from where it had once stood to various places around the world.

Three beach communities had basically been wiped out. Twin Palms had gotten hit the worst, but Ivy thought that was simply because it was the oldest. The other places had been built with better materials to withstand high winds and rain.

She'd told her tale to her family, and Tesla had taken the stage to tell Ivy all about staying at Sweet Breeze during the hurricane. "It was so weird," her niece had said. "The hurricane hit at like eleven o'clock in the morning, but it was really dark."

Ivy had just let her talk, enjoying the air conditioning, the hot chocolate Iris made for her, and the soft bed she'd been able to sleep in.

But now, she wanted her own place.

"Gotta get a job," she muttered to herself. If she wanted to be able to pay rent, she'd have to work.

She showered and headed out, glad she was able to get her car back easily from Mason. In fact, she hadn't even spoken to him. Eden had marched down to the apartment building where he lived and spoken to Henley herself. Ivy had the car twenty minutes later, and her sister had filled it up with gas for her.

She spent the day filling out applications on her phone for a few places around the island, eating tacos in the shade, and watching the waves relentlessly roll ashore. She should go help in the communities that had been devastated by the storm, but she didn't have the heart.

Last year, after the tsunami that had wiped out Orchid's cruise ship, she and Maine had gotten right to work in the affected areas of the island. But Ivy wasn't as good as Orchid, and she knew it.

At this point, though, even a pedicure or a new pair of shoes wouldn't cheer her up.

She wanted to see Mason. Explain everything to him and find out if the connection she'd felt with him out on Long Bar Island could endure here in Getaway Bay.

She knew where he lived, but short of going down there and loitering outside his building, she didn't know how to contact him.

Her phone chimed, and a message came in from

Tidal Cleaning, a play on words for Total Cleaning. *We'd love to speak with you. When are you available?*

Ivy didn't really want to be a maid, but she thought of sharing her room with a nine-year-old and typed out a quick, *Great. I'm available any time.* That totally made her sound desperate, but she didn't care.

At this point, she *was* desperate.

We're over at the clean-up going on in the beach communities. You want to come over?

No, Ivy did not want to go over there. But she knew Twin Palms was mostly cleaned up now. A map for a new dog park had even been circulating on the community's social media page.

I can be there in ten minutes, she said, though it was really more like two. She sighed as she got behind the wheel of her car and made the short drive. She parked in the dirt lot indicated by the volunteer in the orange vest, and she slicked her palms down her shorts as she walked toward the blue tent where the volunteers gathered to get assignments.

"I'm looking for June Iverson," she said without looking at the people there. "She...texted me." She bent to sign her name on the clipboard.

"June's over in Tropical," the man said, and Ivy's heart did a full-stop. The pen scratched on the paper. She lifted her eyes to that pair she had memorized.

So dark. So mesmerizing. So perfect.

"Mason?" He wasn't wearing the cowboy hat, but

he still had a commanding charisma around him that dared her to defy him.

"Ivy." A smile bloomed across his face, though she couldn't fathom why. He glanced at the other person under the tent. A woman. "I'll be back in a sec, Trish." He stepped out of the tent and indicated that Ivy should walk with him.

"How are you?"

"How am I?" she repeated. "My house got blown off the planet. How would you be?"

Mason's hand slipped into hers, but she pulled away. "You know what? I thought I wanted to see you. Explain everything to you. But I don't. I'm...."

Embarrassed.

But she couldn't say the word. What she knew was she didn't belong with him. He was everything she wasn't, right down to the freaking leather shoes he wore to work on the beach.

"Ivy," he said. "I'm sorry it took me a few days to get to you. I found where Orchid lives, and I was going to come by tonight."

"Please, don't."

"Why not?" He reached for her again. "I know you just said that stuff on the island because you didn't want to tell Justin about us." His eyebrows went up. "Right?"

"I mean, I guess."

"You guess?"

"I don't think we're a match, Mase." Even as she said his nickname, she felt like she was lying.

"Why not?"

"Just because I was the only one who applied doesn't make us soul mates."

He looked at the ground and nodded. "All right. Fine. But what if you weren't the only one who applied?"

Confusion raced through Ivy. "You said I was the only one."

"The only one that came through. For some reason, all the others didn't."

"How many others?"

"A couple hundred."

For some reason, the number punched Ivy in the gut. Here she'd thought she was special. But Mason literally had hundreds to choose from. Or he would have, if the messages had come through. Was he lying?

She squinted at him, as if that would help her know.

"Look," he said with a sigh. "I don't know where I belong. I felt like I should leave Texas, so I did. I came here, and being here felt wrong. I bought that island, and concocted this crazy scenario, and you actually did it." He chuckled, but she wasn't sure he'd said anything funny.

In fact, it sounded like he'd called her crazy.

"And I still don't know where I should be," he said.

"But when I think of you, I'm calm, and I think maybe…I belong with you."

Ivy's heart warmed at the thought, but her brain screeched out a warning. "Maybe you should figure that out," she said, tipping up onto her toes and touching his collar. "Because I'll give you my whole heart, Mason Martin, and I don't want it back crushed."

She fell back a step. "Now, if you'll excuse me, I have to go see June about a job. I'm homeless and unemployed. Some of us have to work to make ends meet."

Mason grabbed her hand, and surprise pulled through her as he tugged her back. "Marry me," he said. "You'll have a home, and you won't have to work."

She burst out laughing. "Marry you? You really are crazy." She searched his face, and he certainly looked sane. She shook her hand out of his, fear rising through her chest.

All she'd ever wanted was a man to love her. Cherish her. Take care of her. Why was it now scaring her to death?

"I'm not marrying you."

"Right now? Or ever?" Mason pulled his phone from his back pocket. "If you give me your number, I'll ask you out properly." He took a step closer and leaned down, breaking the bubble of her personal space. "I'll show you we belong together."

"You just said you don't even know where you

belong." Ivy held her ground, though. Didn't back up. Didn't even want to. The ground felt like it might vanish beneath her feet at any moment, and still she didn't move.

"Your number?"

"I don't have it memorized."

"Then give me your phone."

Stupidly, because his nearness and his cologne did things to her mind to make it slow, she handed him her phone. He typed something on it, and a moment later, his phone dinged. "Got it. Good luck with the interview, Ivy."

With that, he walked back to the blue tent, leaving Ivy to wonder what in the world had just happened.

"He proposed to you?" Iris dropped the plate she'd been washing in the sink, creating an ear-splitting clatter that had Ivy shying away from the kitchen. "Where? When? What did he say?"

"It was so unromantic," Ivy said. "Right on the beach where all the debris was. And it was like he grabbed my hand and shouted it at me."

Iris wiped her hands deliberately on a towel. "I'm just going to ask you this one time, twinnie." She lifted her eyes to Ivy's. "Are you in love with him?"

"No," Ivy said with a scoff. She sobered as she flopped onto the couch. "I mean, maybe I liked him a lot out on the island. But we're not out there anymore, are we? I'm not just going to marry some dude I met three weeks ago."

"Mm hmm," Iris said. "The rest of us did."

"Not true. Eden dated Holden way before she met him on Bald Mountain Cliffs."

"Are you going to go out with him?"

"You know what?" Ivy asked. "If he asks me, yes, I'll go out with him."

"So you do like him."

"Of course I like him" Ivy said while rolling her eyes. "He's handsome, and smart, and rich. But he's more than that too." She gazed at nothing as Iris went back to the dishes in the sink. "He doesn't mind that I like to shop. And he doesn't care how many pairs of shoes I have, which for the record, is two, now that all of my stuff is gone. He doesn't mind that I talk a lot."

"Honey, you should've said yes." Iris laughed, and Justin came inside, bringing the scent of grilled meat with him.

"Time to eat," he said. "Hey, baby." He stepped over to Iris and wrapped her in those muscled arms.

She squealed and giggled before saying, "Justin, we're not alone."

"Oh, hey, Ivy," he said without letting go of Iris. "Staying for dinner?"

"I was here when you went outside to grill," she said in a deadpan. "So yeah."

"Is she sleeping over?" he asked in a stage whisper, a teasing grin on his face.

"No," Iris said. "She found a new place today."

"And a job," Ivy said, heaving herself off the couch to join them in the kitchen. "So there." She picked up a plate and started slathering mayonnaise and mustard on her hamburger bun.

Her phone chimed, and she took it out of her pocket and set it on the counter so she could read the text and prepare her dinner. Her heart began pounding. She couldn't read fast enough.

"And a date," she said, and Iris stepped over to her.

Another squeal filled the air, this time as both twins joined their voices together.

Iris grabbed the phone before Ivy even knew what was happening. "Yes," she dictated as she typed. "I'd love to go out with you, Mason."

"Iris," Ivy said. "Not love. Just say *sure, when?*"

"Sure, when?" Iris barley looked at her before she focused back on the phone. "Nope, that doesn't work."

"I thought you liked Mason," Justin said, cracking an egg into a hot pan, which resulted in a hiss. "Was there any question of you two going out?"

"Yes," Ivy said. "He's...honestly, I'm not sure what he is. He doesn't even know what he wants or where he belongs."

"Sent," Iris said, and Ivy's stomach dropped to the ground. No way it had taken that long to type *sure, when?*

"That's easy, Ivy," Justin said. "You tell him he belongs with you."

That was the second time that day someone had said that to her. She didn't know what to make of it, but happiness filled her when another chime came from her phone.

"Right," she said sarcastically. "Then he'd be here eating your food, too."

She picked up her phone and saw Iris had sent the *I'd love to go out with you* text.

Great, Mason had messaged back. *What are you doing right now?*

CHAPTER SIXTEEN

*M*ason sat in his car outside the sushi restaurant Ivy had said was her favorite. He was still trying to acquire a taste for raw fish, but he hadn't told her that. He'd have done almost anything to see her again, and if he had to pretend to like a red dragon roll to do it, he would.

But he knew he wouldn't have to pretend. If he didn't like sushi, Ivy wouldn't care. At least he hoped she wouldn't. They'd had plenty of differences on the island, and they'd gotten along fine then.

He'd given no thought to what would happen to their relationship once they got back to the island, because Mason didn't like to think more than a few days ahead. Maybe a week. But his momma had taught him not to worry too far into the future, because things changed.

The tropical storm had certainly changed a lot for

Mason out on Long Bar Island. And as he'd had time over the last few days alone to think about what had exactly changed, he knew what the biggest change had been: himself.

And those changes had allowed him to see Ivy in a completely new light.

A knock sounded on his passenger window, and he yelped as he twisted toward in that direction.

Ivy's beautiful face filled the window, and he hurried to unlock the car, thinking he'd get out. Instead, she got in.

"Wow," she said, looking around. "What kind of car is this?" She briefly met his eye. "I pegged you for a guy with a pickup truck."

"I have one of those too," he said, his lungs not quite expanding properly. "This is some fancy sports car the salesman said I'd like."

"And do you like it?" She reached out and stroked the dashboard as if the car would purr under her touch.

"It's nice with the top down," he admitted. "Driving along the coast."

"Let's do that," Ivy said.

"You don't want to eat?"

"I ate just before you texted." She looked at him then, apprehension in those lovely eyes.

Mason needed to erase that. "You should've just told me."

"I just did." Her eyes slid down his body. "You look great in regular clothes."

"Thanks." He allowed himself a moment to take in the bright blue tank top she wore, with the tiny pair of white shorts. "So do you." He flipped the car into reverse. "So we're driving."

His stomach wasn't happy about that, but he could feed it later.

"Do you know the road that goes out by the cattle ranch?" she asked.

"Yep," he said. "I've worked out there a few times."

"Oh, right," she said. "You said that on the island."

Mason had told her that, and a lot of other things. And he had more to say, which surprised even him. "I'm not going to leave Getaway Bay," he said.

"Is that right?"

"Yeah," he said. "See, I kind of did this crazy thing. I bought a deserted island and I put out an ad to find someone to come live on it with me for a few months."

"Fascinating." Ivy ran her hands through her hair as Mason pressed the button to put the top down. The breeze picked up, especially as he drove out of town, away from all the businesses, all the tourists, all the pressures of real life.

"Yeah," he said. "It was interesting. My servers went down almost immediately, and it took several days for all the messages that had come in to cache and then send them over."

Beside him, Ivy stiffened, but he continued anyway. "By then, I'd left the island. See, just one message made it through. I'm not sure how. My IT guys aren't sure either. They think it came in at just the right moment, and it was a fluke."

"A fluke," she echoed, her voice almost a whisper.

Mason gathered his courage close and reached across the console to take her hand in his. "I don't think it was a fluke. I think it was fate. Ivy McLaughlin, I belong with you."

Ivy said nothing, but she didn't pull her hand away. Mason maneuvered them around the curves in the island, the beach on his left, and the woman of his dreams on his right.

"I'm sorry about your house," he said. "What have you decided to do?" He glanced at her and caught her wiping her eyes.

Feeling helpless, he pulled to the side of the road. "Hey," he said. "What's wrong? I'm sorry I brought up the house."

"It's not the house," she said, her voice pinched and high. She turned toward him, and she wasn't embarrassed that she was crying. In fact, she looked fierce and determined, while being soft and loveable at the same time. "Do you really think you belong with me?"

"Absolutely."

"That it was really fate?" she asked before he could even finish the word.

"Yes," he said. "Ivy." He cradled her face in his palm. "I started falling in love with you out there."

She glanced down, her chin trembling. She pressed

her lips together and shook her head. "You don't think we're too different?"

"Why would we be too different?"

"Well, I'm jobless and homeless, and you're a billionaire. For one."

"I'll hire you," he said.

"Oh, I got a job," she said with a smile.

"I was going to say you could come live with me too, but I thought you'd say no to that."

"I'll find somewhere," she said. "Now that I have a job."

"What's your job?"

"I got a job with an insurance company," she said. "I went to apply for a maid job, but before I got to the interview, someone needed help with something, and I stepped over to the table to help them with the paperwork."

She tucked her hair behind her ear, and Mason heard the hint of pride in her voice. Ivy came off as confident, but she had a real self-conscious streak too.

"And the agent hired me on the spot. Said I could start immediately, and I did." She shrugged like it was no big deal. "I'm a good secretary."

"I'm sure you are," he said, glad she felt good about herself. "And I could use someone like you."

"I'd be your girlfriend," she said, and Mason really liked the sound of that. He pulled back onto the road and kept driving, his heart filling with happiness.

"I'm starving," he said when he rounded the curve

and saw the Cattleman's Last Stop ahead. "Would you sit with me while I eat?"

"Oh, if we're stopping here, I'm in," she said. "They have the best sweet potato fries."

Mason couldn't imagine why anyone would like sweet potato fries more than regular ones, but he just smiled as he pulled his fancy sports car into the gravel parking lot and found a space.

Ivy ran her fingers through her hair before getting out of the car, and Mason drew her right into his arms. "I missed you, Ivy," he murmured, touching his mouth to her cheek, closer to her ear than anything else.

"Mm." She pressed into him. "It was a rough transition back to island life, wasn't it?"

He chuckled, his mind still thinking about one thing: kissing her. "Is that what you call this? Island life?"

"Yes," she said, reaching up and slipping his cowboy hat from his head. "Maybe that's why you haven't liked living on the island so far. You're not doing it right."

"And you'll show me how to do it right?"

"Yeah." She grinned at him.

"Deal." With that, he leaned down and kissed her, the thrill of it just as magical as the first time.

SEVERAL DAYS LATER, MASON ONCE AGAIN picked up Ivy in his ritzy car. His nerves had been pinging him for hours, but he knew he looked good on the outside.

Ivy ran her hands down the blue and orange plaid shirt he'd chosen and smiled. "Nice."

"Yeah?"

She adjusted his hat and beamed up at him. "It's just my sister."

"Your *twin* sister," Mason said.

"Are you scared to meet her?"

"Out of my mind scared," he said.

"You've already met Justin," she said. "And he's more protective of me than Iris."

"You've mentioned that," he said. "Why is that?"

"I don't know," Ivy said. "But he really wants all of us McLaughlin's to be happy. He takes care of my parents' yard now and everything."

Mason nodded, trying not to be jealous. When Ivy had spoken about her relationship with her brother-in-law, Mason hadn't been sure about it. He'd thought maybe Justin had fallen in love with both twins, as Iris was identical to Ivy.

"Only in looks," Ivy had told him a few times over the past week since they'd taken their drive down the coast, eaten hamburgers, and gotten back together.

She'd started her new job, and Mason had been picking her up each evening so they could spend time together. No, they weren't on the sand. Weren't eating oatmeal or trying to fix a radio in the middle of the night.

But Mason liked her just as much as he had out on Long Bar Island, pedicures and cute wedges and everything. And she seemed to like him too, though she teased him about what he did all day as a retired thirty-five-year-old.

He was still trying to figure that out himself, but he knew he would. He'd spoken to the Holstein's about their ranch, and he'd looked into buying something himself. On the island, there were avocado farms, macadamia nut farms, pineapple plantations, and plenty of other places that echoed a cattle ranch.

Ivy could do his books, as she'd said once, and Mason was seriously considering doing something. That would get him out of the high-rise apartment he didn't like. He needed land to call his. Somewhere to look over and feel proud about.

"I have a confession," he said as she buckled her seatbelt.

"Oh, this is going to be good," Ivy said in a teasing voice.

"I've been looking to buy a farm or something."

"Oh." Surprise coated the word now. "What kind?"

"I don't know. There are actually a couple of options, and I'm wondering if you'd come look at them with me next week."

"I'd like that," she said.

Relief filled him. She hadn't laughed. Hadn't said he should just enjoy retirement—what his older brother had said when Mason had called Donald to talk about it.

He'd said, "It's your money, Mason. Do what you want with it. But I'd love to be retired. You should enjoy it."

Mason had had almost a year without working, and he couldn't say he'd enjoyed it. Sure, there were brief moments of happiness, especially with Ivy in his life now. But he liked working. He liked looking at before and after pictures of barns and land and homes and seeing the improvement his hard work had accomplished. Great satisfaction came to him through hard work, making things look better, function better, produce better.

Ivy chattered about a new friend at work, and Mason listened to her while navigating according to his GPS's directions. When they finally pulled into her sister's house in a quiet suburb up in the hills, Mason felt more relaxed.

Another blonde woman came out onto the porch before he could get out of the car, and Ivy said, "There she is."

Justin joined them, his arm slipping easily around Iris, and all of Mason's fears about the other man disappeared.

Ivy faced him. "Ready?"

"So ready." He got out of the car and waved to the couple on the porch before hurrying around the back of the car to help Ivy out of the car. It was low to the ground, and she wore high heels and had a hard time getting out without him.

He liked that she needed him, that she *wanted* to rely on him. "Hey," she said. "Iris, this is Mason. Mason, you know Justin. And this is Ivy, my twin sister."

"Good to see you again, man," Justin said.

"Mason," Iris said, her voice a note or two high on the false scale. "I've heard so much about you."

"Likewise." He shook Justin's hand when he reached the top of the steps, and then Iris's.

"Come in," Justin said. "We have dinner almost ready." He went inside, and Iris flashed a look in Ivy's direction that Mason didn't miss.

He followed Justin though, leaving the twins to talk if they wanted to. Because he knew who he was—and more importantly, *Ivy* knew who he was.

CHAPTER SEVENTEEN

*I*vy hummed as she rinsed the dishes in Orchid's sink. No, she didn't have a place of her own yet. She did have a job, and she and Mason would be going to look at an avocado farm later that day, after she got off work.

She'd considered not getting a place of her own, but she hadn't told anyone that yet. She tended to make major life plans before she should, and she and Mason hadn't had a discussion about marriage yet.

But she was thinking that she'd just hang here with Orchid until she and Mason got married. Then she could move in with him....

But she also knew she wanted a big, splashy wedding—and those took time to plan.

"But when Orchid marries Maine, her house will be empty...." She mused. And Orchid wouldn't want to give it up, Ivy knew that. She and her first husband had lived here for a couple of years before his death, and Orchid had been raising Tesla here.

"So talk to her about it tonight," Ivy told the now-clean sink. If she could stay here until the wedding in December, and even beyond, she would.

After all, Mason had not declared his love for her while they drove along the coast last week. Yes, he'd said he belonged with her, and she felt the same about him.

But there had been no *I love you*'s exchanged. She should probably hear that before she started planning nuptials.

With the dishes done, she grabbed her purse and headed out to her car.

She didn't mind her job at the insurance office, but she didn't love it either. She didn't know what she would love. Probably not working, but she'd never been in a position where she didn't have to work.

Plus, she had a new friend in the office, and Bri was fun and fresh and she reminded Ivy so much of her former self.

She knew where all the parties were happening, and who had gone out with who lately, and which jeans would get a man to look her way even on the beach.

Ivy liked talking to her, but she hadn't run right out to get new jeans or added any social events to her calendar. She spent her evenings with Mason, usually with a lot of silence, the scent of his cologne, and something sweet to eat while she told him about her day and he kissed her like his life depended on having his mouth against hers.

Maybe she was reading too much into their evenings together, but she didn't think so. And tonight, they were going to look at two places back-to-back. She was secretly hoping the avocado farm would be better than the macadamia nut orchards, because she'd heard horror stories about the mess those trees made.

"Morning, Bri," she said when she got to the office.

The brunette rose from her desk, which sat just inside the front door. She met every person who came to the real estate office, and she had the perfect face and personality for it.

"Yes or no question," she said. "Are you seriously dating Mason Martin? The cowboy billionaire?"

"That's two questions," Ivy said with a smile.

"They're the same question," Bri said, following Ivy through the door and into the inner offices. Ivy put her purse on her desk, the first one there. She basically handled reimbursements for roadside assistance and other issues, and the job wasn't busy but it had started to pay some of her bills.

"Yes," Ivy said.

"He was the guy who bought Long Bar Island."

"Yes," Ivy said as if she hadn't anticipated this conversation. But Mason had made Internet headlines with his ad, and Ivy was surprised nothing had come out about his return to Getaway Bay earlier than anticipated.

"Did you go out there with him?" Bri sat in the chair opposite of Ivy's desk, her dark eyes shining like stars. "Just warning you, if you say yes, I'm going to lose my mind."

"Oh, I can't have that happen," Ivy said, sitting down in front of her computer.

"That's a freaking yes!" Bri sucked in a breath and let out a squeal, apparently the noise she made when losing her mind.

"Did you know me and at least ten of my friends sent him a message and he never answered?"

"Wow." Ivy cemented her smile in place. She couldn't help the feeling of inadequacy that moved through her. If Mason had met or seen a picture of Bri, she felt certain that he'd have chosen her over Ivy.

But there was no way to know for sure. Mason hadn't gotten any of those messages. But that voice of doubt in the back of Ivy's mind whispered, *Did he pick you because you were the only one who responded?*

"Girl, I can't believe you didn't tell me this," Bri said.

"It's…nothing," Ivy said. "We experienced some turbulence out on the island, and we're obviously back before the three months ended."

"Obviously," Bri said, leaning her elbows on Ivy's desk, settling in for the story Ivy didn't want to tell. "So tell me what happened."

Ivy looked past her computer to her friend sitting

across from her. "You know what? I fell in love with him. That's what happened."

And it was absolutely true—and she wanted to tell Mason right now.

She picked up her purse and put her hand inside as if looking for her phone. Her fingers touched it and she pushed the volume button on the side to make it chime.

"Oh," she said as if surprised she'd gotten the text. She pulled the phone from her purse and added, "I need to make a call."

Bri followed her out into the lobby saying, "I see how it is."

Ivy tapped Mason's name and then the phone icon, moving the device to her ear as she continued outside. Bri would have dozens more questions, but Ivy didn't want to deal with them right then.

"Hey, beautiful," Mason said, filling Ivy with the bravery she needed.

"Mase," she said, her voice suddenly dying. "I...." She glanced around the parking lot in front of her. "I realized something just now, and I wanted to tell you."

"Okay," he said, sounded distracted.

"I love you." She giggled, mostly because her nerves were screaming a warning at her. She turned in a circle, suddenly wanting the world to know. "I'm in love with you."

A noise came through the line, and then utter silence.

"That's all," Ivy said, her voice little more than a squeak now. "I'll see you tonight."

"Wait," he barked as if she'd hang up immediately.

She waited.

"I love you, too."

"Oh, Mase, you don't have to say it just because I did."

"I'm not," he said. "I'm coming to you now."

"You don't need—"

"Ivy," he said very calmly. "I need to look into your eyes and make sure you hear me."

"I can hear you."

"I don't think you can. You're at work already?"

"Yes."

"See you in ten." The line went dead, as if he expected her to continue to argue with him.

Ivy dropped her hand from her ear, the phone clutched tightly in her fingers.

I love you, too.

Was that true?

She sat down on the bench in front of the insurance office, thinking ten minutes would take an hour to pass.

Before she knew it, Mason pulled up in his fancy dark blue pickup truck, that delectable cowboy hat perched perfectly on his head.

She stood as he got out, not even bothering to park or turn off the truck. He possessed an intensity she loved, and he didn't say hello before taking her face in both of his hands and saying, "I'm in love with you, Ivy."

Emotion filled her, and tears pricked her eyes. She'd already said it, and her voice felt too weak to do so again.

Mason kissed her, and that was all the reassurance she needed that he'd spoken true.

"Does this mean you'll talk to me about getting married now?" he asked, resting his forehead against hers.

Ivy smiled, a laugh spilling from her lips. "Yes," she said. "We can start talking about that."

THE SUMMER SLIPPED AWAY WHILE IVY planned the wedding she wanted to have. She kept her designs in a thick binder in Orchid's kitchen cupboard, and she tried not to get it out when her sister was home.

Orchid wanted to marry Maine, but football season had started up again, and she was back on the sidelines with him. Not really, but he had a publicist who wanted a say in everything about the wedding, and Orchid was ready to charter a flight with her fiancé and island hop until she found someone who would just marry them.

"Then the media and the people of Getaway Bay

won't have a say in what kind of blasted cake we eat," she'd said to him on the phone just the other night.

Ivy tried to tell her that Maine was a celebrity in Getaway Bay, but Orchid knew that. So she'd just commiserated with her sister and tried to support her if she could.

One Friday afternoon, she'd left work early so she could go meet with the wedding planner Mason had generously paid for.

Your Tidal Forever put together the absolute best weddings on the island, and Ivy had wanted a planner there for as long as she could remember.

And now she had Charlotte Dawson building a one-of-a-kind altar for her and Mason's beach wedding.

Ivy had decided she wanted everyone to sail out to Long Bar Island, where she and Mason would be married. They'd serve dinner on the yacht on the way there, followed by a reception aboard the boat once they got back to the dock.

Family only—his and hers. Friends and acquaintances could come to the reception at the yacht club, and Charlotte needed access to the yacht to see about some décor she'd been planning.

Her phone rang, and Ivy picked up her sister's call. "Heya, Eden."

"Are you working today?" Her sister's voice sounded panicked and full of pain.

"No, what's wrong?"

"My water broke."

Ivy jumped her feet, searching the room for something. What, she didn't know. Her keys. Something.

"Where's Holden?"

"Oh, he has a meeting."

"Eden," Ivy said, finally locating her keys and swiping them from the desk. "You're having his baby. Call him right now. I'm on my way to the hospital."

"Come pick me up," she said, groaning. Ivy waited until she quieted. "I'm at home."

"Okay," Ivy said. "I'll call everyone."

"All right," Eden said. "But I don't want anyone in the delivery room but Holden."

"We know, Eden," Ivy said, though she would give almost anything to be there and be the first one to hold Eden's baby. Oh, how Ivy wanted babies.

And she and Mason would be married within the month, and maybe she'd get her chance to be a wife and mother—all she'd ever wanted.

As she pulled out of Orchid's driveway, she said, "Dial Orchid, my sister."

When the call connected, she said, "Orchid, Eden's having the baby!"

And she'd never been happier that she'd been the first to know this news and could make all the necessary calls to her family.

CHAPTER EIGHTEEN

*M*ason adjusted his tie, the purple paisley something he actually liked. Over the last several months, he'd spent plenty of time with Ivy's family, something else he really loved. He loved his family too, and they'd be on the island in just a few short weeks when he married Ivy.

But the McLaughlin's had a different kind of relationship he'd never experienced before. Everything had been set for his marriage to Ivy for a few weeks now, but Ivy would not get married before Orchid.

"She's been waiting forever," Ivy had told him while they lay in each other's arms on the sand. "And she'll be upset if we get married before her."

"It's fine," Mason said, though he was tired of watching Ivy leave his apartment at night or kissing her under the porch light at Orchid's house before she went in.

"Looks good," Justin said as he stepped up to the mirror where Mason stood. "You ready to do this in a couple of weeks?"

"Definitely," Mason said.

"You ever been married?" Justin asked.

"Nope." A tremor of fear slipped through him, but he reminded himself that he was marrying Ivy, and he loved her. She loved him, and not because he'd taken her out to a deserted island and tried to make a love connection.

They'd been back to Long Bar Island a couple of times since then, just for the day. Mason always made sure Justin, Holden, and Ivy's father knew they were going and to come get them if they didn't return by nightfall.

Of course, there hadn't been any other problems. Thankfully. He didn't like the feeling of being stranded, and he'd definitely had it the best out of any of the new brothers-in-law he'd be getting very soon.

Maine entered the room, his father right behind him. Mason had met the star quarterback several times, and he grinned at the man. "It's here," he said.

"Finally." Maine smiled around at everyone, and he simply oozed charisma. "We got Orchid moved out last night, too. So you're good to move in."

"Oh, I won't do that until I get married." Mason looked at his own reflection again. "And we're keeping the apartment too." He wasn't sure why he didn't want to let go of it. He liked looking out the windows at the beach, especially as the sun rose. Though there wasn't an ocean in his part of Texas, for some reason, watching the sun rise over the waves reminded him of the ranch he'd sold.

He and Ivy had spent a lot of time in his apartment, and he wanted to keep it. He owned it, as he'd bought it with cash, and he didn't see a reason to get rid of it yet.

"I hear your wedding is going to outshine this one," Maine said as he held out his arm for his dad to put in the cufflinks. Holden came out of the dressing room, decked out in his matching suit.

"Nah," Mason said. "We're just serving dinner on the yacht as we sail out to the island. Then we'll get married on the beach. Snap a few pictures. And get back on the boat."

"Sounds pretty amazing," he said.

"Have you seen how many cameras are outside?" Holden asked. "This is the event of the year on this island."

Maine's face stormed for a moment, and then he sighed. "I suppose it is. But you guys are getting married next year, so maybe that will be the event of the year too."

Mason simply smiled and shook his head. "I doubt it. We only invited family and a couple of close family friends." Ivy's parents had long-time friends on the island, and she'd wanted them to come. Other than that, it was her siblings and their spouses, and his parents and his two brothers and their families.

Donald and Elliott had both been married for years, and he had six nieces and nephews back in Texas.

"It's time," a man said from the doorway, and Mason gave one final tug on his tie. He didn't spend a lot of time wearing such formal clothing, and everything felt like it was pulling just a little bit.

Maine got escorted by two men and his father down a side hallway, where he disappeared through a door that would take him to the front of the church where he and Orchid were getting married.

Mason went with Holden and Justin, and they all paired up with the appropriate McLaughlin sister. Ivy ogled him as he walked toward her, pure delight in her eyes.

"Wow," she said as he linked his fingers with hers. "Don't you look all fancy?"

"Do I?" he asked, refusing to reach up and smooth his tie again. "You look great too."

Orchid had chosen a soft pink for her bridesmaid's dresses, and they were beautiful. Ivy wore rhinestones around her neck and dripping from her earlobes, and her hair had been piled on top of her head in a delicate arrangement that almost looked like flowers.

He leaned over and touched his lips to hers. "I can't wait until this is us," he said.

"Yeah, except it'll be way less formal than this," she said.

"And you want that, right?"

"Of course." She slipped her hand into the crook of his arm as the music started playing, and the wedding party started advancing toward the doors and down the aisle. Mason didn't like having so many eyes on him, but he held his head high and kept his feet moving where they were supposed to go.

This wasn't his wedding yet, but he felt the heightened nerves from Maine as Orchid finally appeared, her wedding dress pure white and ballooning out from her body. Love and happiness filled the air when she reached Maine's side and he swept a kiss across her cheek, murmuring something to her.

Mason couldn't help watching Ivy, and he caught her looking at him several times too. He couldn't imagine anyone else at his side, and while he still didn't know why his servers had gone down all those months ago, he didn't care.

Maybe the god of technology had known exactly what he was doing, and Mason wasn't going to doubt it.

THE WEEKS PASSED, AND FINALLY, HE FOUND himself meeting the chef Ivy had hired to cook their wedding dinner at the dock. "Tadashi?" he asked, taking in the Hawaiian man lifting a box out of his trunk.

"You must be Mason." The man shook hands with Mason and nodded to the car. "I have more in there."

"Great." Mason collected a box as well, and they walked over to the dock where the yacht waited. "Ivy said you'd need access about eight o'clock tomorrow morning."

"That's right," Tadashi said. "That way, we can eat when we set sail at one."

And the wedding would be at three, right after they arrived and made it ashore on Long Bar Island. Ivy had been out to the beach with her sisters yesterday, and she wouldn't tell him what she'd done out there. She'd strictly forbidden him from going out to see, and they'd planned to spend today together so he wouldn't be able to sneak away.

He could only hope whatever she'd done out there wouldn't get stripped away by the wind, and that the rain would hold off for another couple of days. After that, Mother Nature could unleash anything she wanted.

He helped Tadashi unload all of his equipment, and he answered the chef's questions about the kitchen and dining arrangements. Mason had hired a company to come put in another table so their living area could be used as well, and there was now a leaf between that table and the existing dining room table.

Extra chairs had been brought in, and Ivy's wedding planner would be arriving tonight to get everything decorated and set for the wedding. She'd given Charlotte a keycard for the dock, and Mason handed one to Tadashi now.

"This should get you into the dock," he said. "And then you just come aboard."

"Thanks." Tadashi fiddled around with dials and opened cupboards while Mason looked down the long table. Ivy's family would take up sixteen seats, and that included her family and friends, an aunt and two cousins.

His family was just eleven, and with the two of them, that made twenty-nine people. It certainly looked like enough room, and he went back out into the winter sunshine.

Tadashi joined him several minutes later, and they left the dock together.

The next time Mason boarded his yacht, Justin and Maine had created a wall of flesh in front of him so he couldn't see more than six inches in front of his face. Ivy didn't want him to see her in her dress until a few minutes before departure, and she'd hired a photographer to get the "first look."

They led him down to his cabin, and he glanced at the one closest to the kitchen where he and Ivy had slept while they waited for someone to come help them. A rush of memories hit him, and he realized he was getting married that day.

Married.

His mother was already in the cabin, and Justin and Maine left him there with them to get ready. "Hey, Ma."

He hugged her, so glad she'd made the trip though it had been difficult for her.

"My boy is getting married." She was already crying, and Mason just smiled at her.

"Hard to believe, isn't it?"

"Not at all. And Ivy is so nice." Her Texas twang made everything sound so country, and Mason liked it.

"Your dress is pretty," he said, hanging up his tuxedo in the slim closet.

"Jamie helped me pick it out."

Donald's wife, who had been taking care of Mason's mother the most since Don and Elliott had taken over the ranch together.

"Ivy said I could go help her," she said, stepping to the door. "I just wanted to see you." She stretched up and kissed his cheek, and Mason watched her leave.

Then he got himself dressed for the wedding, doing his own cufflinks as he didn't have a father to help him. A strong sense of missing hit him, but he didn't let it linger for too long. He knew his father was there in spirit.

Elliott entered the room several minutes later, his face lit up. "Ready?"

"Are they ready for me?"

He nodded. "The photographer is right here, and she wants to talk to you before you go up."

A brunette entered the cabin, a camera hanging at her side from a strap. "I'm Erin. Okay," she said. "For the first look, you'll stand right where I tell you.

174

You'll turn when I say, and this is the most important part."

She paused, and Mason didn't have the remotest desire to disobey this woman. "You have to smile. You have to act like the dress is the most beautiful thing you've ever seen, even if you hate it."

"Will I hate it?" Mason looked from her to Elliott.

"I'm sure you won't," Erin said. "But you have to smile and be happy, no matter what."

Mason couldn't see why he wouldn't be, but she must've had problems like this in the past. So he simply nodded. She did too, and then she turned and led him out of the cabin. "Groom coming," she called down the narrow halls, and a door closed up ahead.

Ivy's cabin.

Mason kept his eyes straight ahead as they walked past the dining area, which looked like it belonged on a completely different yacht. Tablecloths had been spread, and beautiful flowers sat in vases down the length of the table.

Pictures of him and Ivy hung on the walls, and the opening into the kitchen had been covered by greenery. Pristine china sat on the tables, with champagne flutes and crystal glassware and shiny silverware.

Bells hung from the railings outside, making a twinkling sound as the ship moved through the water on its way toward Long Bar Island.

Flower vines had been woven throughout as well, and Mason smiled at everything.

"Stand here," Erin said, and Mason did as she said. "Face the water." He was aware of movement behind him, of people talking, of things happening. But he kept his eyes out on the water, the foaming waves the yacht left behind.

Erin appeared in front of him. "Okay, she's in position. You're going to wait to move until I say." She smiled at him, her dark eyes firing. "And you're so happy, remember?"

"So happy," Mason repeated, and he was. His heart pounded in his chest. Ivy had not told him a single thing about her wedding gown, other than that it was "perfect."

So he better act like it.

"All right," Erin said from behind him. "Turn slowly, Mason. Slowly."

He did, his nerves making him tug on the end of his jacket sleeves. Though it was January, and there was definitely a nippy breeze on the boat, he felt sweaty from head to toe. The sun did shine overhead, and Mason thanked the weather for cooperating.

Erin's camera went *click click click* as Mason's eyes met Ivy's. She beamed like the brightest star in the sky, and Mason drank in the beauty of her, a slow smile stretching his mouth.

"Wow," he said, taking a step toward her.

"Slow," Erin called. "Everything is done slowly."

Ivy's dress hugged her curves and fell off her shoulders in an appealing, sexy way. It went all the way to the floor, and it seemed to glisten in the sunlight. As he got closer and his fingers tingled in anticipation of touching her, he saw it was covered with lace and beads that reflected the light.

"You're stunning," he said, the words almost sticking in his throat.

"You clean up nice yourself," Ivy said.

"Kiss her," Erin said. "Slow, like you've done before. No pucker."

Mason did what he was told, and every cell in his body rejoiced that this woman was about to be his.

CHAPTER NINETEEN

$\mathcal{I}$vy laughed as she and Mason sat last at the head of the dinner table. Everyone had fit, and Charlotte had worked her magic on the decorations. Several of her assistants came out of the small kitchen bearing the first course, an endive salad with a bacon-wrapped scallop.

She'd opted for the surf and turf menu from Tadashi, who was the premier wedding chef on the island.

They'd spent thirty minutes taking pictures, and then Charlotte had held them on the upper deck while everyone else took their places for dinner. Then everyone had applauded as they'd come in, which seemed odd, as they hadn't even gotten married yet.

"This is great," Mason said, a measure of surprise in his voice.

"You thought it wouldn't be?"

"It's green," he said with a grin, and Ivy fell in love with him a little bit more in that very moment.

Chatter began as everyone got served and dinner truly began. She'd told her dad he could give the opening speech once they docked and the reception began. That too was taking place on the yacht, and their guests would board the ship for refreshments and to wish her and Mason well.

Ivy barely tasted the food. She felt every swell of water beneath the boat, but she'd hired a captain so Mason wouldn't have to navigate them to the island and back. She loved being in the spotlight, but there was something equally as terrifying about it.

Just as the dessert plates got cleared, the ship slowed. "We're here." She met Mason's eyes, and his sparked with just as much nervous energy as hers.

"I love you," he said, his reminder that they would be able to survive anything. He took her hand and stood, gently drawing her out into the open air, where they faced the island together.

She and her sisters had come out a couple of days ago with more of the flowering vines Charlotte had bought for the wedding. The designer had come too, and they'd wrapped the tree trunks with flowers and bells.

The altar waited right where Charlotte had put it, and all of the chairs they'd anchored in the sand still stood.

"Ivy," Mason said, wonder in his voice. "This is beautiful."

"I love you, too."

It became quite the process to get everyone ashore without dampening dresses, and it wasn't until several long minutes before everyone had found a seat, Mason had taken his place at the altar, and she and her father waited down at the other end of the aisle.

Charlotte planned to play the wedding march from the ship, over the speaker system, but there had obviously been a problem. Ivy glanced at the boat, but she couldn't see the wedding planner.

Eden had just stood up and passed her daughter to Holden when a crackle and a screech came from the speakers on the boat.

"Sorry," Charlotte's voice said next, and it definitely filled the sky. Then the wedding march began, and Ivy fixed her eyes on Mason's as her father escorted her down the aisle to her husband-to-be.

Last New Year's, if someone had told her she'd be getting married the following January, she'd have assumed a different man at the end of the aisle. But Mason was absolutely perfect for her, and she felt like the luckiest woman in the world.

He received her from her father, his grip on her hand sure and strong. They faced the pastor, and Ivy listened as he spoke about the sanctity of marriage and counseled them to be true to one another.

"And I believe you wrote your own vows," he said, looking at Ivy.

She drew in a shaky breath and faced Mason. "Mase, you're everything I didn't know I wanted." She smiled at him, her stomach doing flips. "I love you, and I promise to always put you first in my life and rely on you the way we had to do when we first came to this island."

He remained silent as if she had more to say, but she didn't. "Your turn," she prompted.

He flinched, a quick chuckle following. "I was expecting you to talk longer."

Several people in the crowd giggled too, and then Mason said, "Ivy, you are the perfect woman for me. I belong with you, and I promise to do my best to take care of you, cherish you, and make sure you're happy."

I belong with you.

Ivy liked those words more than *I love you*, and tears pricked the backs of her eyes. She kept them inside so she wouldn't have black makeup running down her face.

The pastor pronounced them husband and wife, and Ivy reached up to take Mason's face in her hands so she could kiss her husband.

He growled in the back of his throat as cheers filled the island paradise around them, and he held her tight as he kissed her back.

Ivy hugged her parents and her sisters, then moved over to Mason's mother. "Thank you for raising such a good man." She hugged Lorraine and her new brothers and sisters-in-law before returning to Mason's side.

Always to Mason's side.

"I love you," he murmured. "Can I put my cowboy hat back on now?"

She tipped her head toward the sky and laughed. "All right, cowboy. But only for the ride back. You have to take it off for the reception too."

"Only for you," he muttered, taking the hat from his brother and positioning it on his head.

He was the most handsome man in the world, and Ivy kissed him again. "I love you, Mase."

"Love you too, Ivy."

Read on for a sneak peek of **THE HEARTWOOD SEA,** a clean contemporary romance!

SNEAK PEEK! THE HEARTWOOD
SEA CHAPTER ONE

*A*lissa Heartwood knew it was time to get up before her alarm even went off. Waking before dawn for the past decade could do that to a person. She had two of the most important jobs for The Heartwood Inn, the family-run hotel, resort, and restaurant on the popular island of Carter's Cove, and they both started in the middle of the night.

One of the very last family-run establishments, the way the big corporations with their big checks and big pens had been coming in. Literally, great big checks that took three people to hold them while cameras clicked.

But Alissa's family had stayed the course, and their "inn" was more of a luxury resort these days, with that downhome family feel people craved, even if they didn't know it.

Alissa's job was to bring in the catch-of-the-day on her

trusty shrimp boat, and everyone knew the best time to get fish was before the sun rose. She didn't mind, as she loved the calmness of the Atlantic Ocean as it got painted with the first rays of glorious, golden sunlight each day.

Well, at least each day in the height of the summer season, which it currently was.

After that, Alissa slicked back her hair into a tight bun and started on the pastries for the day. She'd been professionally trained for four long years of pastry school, and people could come into Heartwood just for their bakery.

Her creations.

Handmade, every morning.

The best part of Alissa's job was that she finished by one o'clock, though most people didn't know that was the end of a ten-hour workday.

Alissa knew it, and her back knew it, and the last of the summer cold she'd been fighting for weeks knew it. Still, she got dressed, not bothering to shower, and whistled for Dodger and Pirate to join her.

She lived in her grandparents' old house, as only her grandmother remained alive now, and she'd moved in with Alissa's parents when they'd officially retired from the Heartwood empire. Alissa's oldest sister, Olympia, ran things now, and Alissa took a moment in the darkness to appreciate everything she had.

Sure, maybe she was lonely at night. Even in the afternoons, boredom found her. She needed a summer boyfriend, but she'd had one of those, thank you very much, and he'd left the island with most of her heart.

She'd tried dating a bit over the winter, but it was a half-hearted attempt, and she knew it. *Half-hearted*. She chuckled at her own lame joke, because it wasn't funny what Calvin had done with her heart, and headed toward the dock across the sand.

Very few houses sat along the beach, as the hurricane season in South Carolina was no joke. But somehow, the Heartwood cottage where her grandparents had raised four daughters and a son had weathered all the storms over the years.

Alissa boarded *Big Blue*, patting the side of the boat like she did every morning. "Morning, Blue," she said to the vessel as if it could respond. "Lots of shrimp today, okay? It's Monday, and we get a lot of families in on Mondays."

Especially if they came before seven, as kids ate free with a paying adult on Mondays. After that, cocktail hour began, and Redfin, the restaurant another of Alissa's sisters managed, became crowded with adults holding delicate flutes of champagne, women wearing slinky dresses and men decked out in polos.

"Maybe I should go to cocktail hour tonight," she said to Dodger, who'd just put his paws up on the doorknob, as if the German shepherd couldn't wait to get inside the steering room. But the dog hated it in there. He'd probably left a ball in the corner somewhere. Alissa wouldn't put it past him; the dog was as smart as they come.

Alissa unlocked the door and let Dodger in. Pirate, a much smaller basset hound, followed. Alissa moved around all the dials and switches with the ease of a seasoned pro. Of course, she *was* a seasoned pro, as she'd been heading out at three a.m. on this boat since she was five years old.

A pang of missing for her grandfather hit her, and she touched two fingers to her lips and said, "Love you, Grandpa," before starting the engine. *Big Blue* groaned, but she came to life, and Alissa's face burst into a smile. "Good girl."

She backed out of the dock, flipped on her lights, and sent up a quick plea for a lot of shrimp. She didn't want to deal with Gwen's attitude about having to buy from the bigger commercial boats if Alissa couldn't bring in enough shrimp.

Of course, it happened. She was one boat, while the commercial fisheries had whole teams of people, boats, and fishing spots. She just had the traps and lines she'd been setting for years now, though it did help that she didn't have to go out as far as they did, and they couldn't come into her waters and poach from her.

Captaining the boat brought Alissa a slip of happiness, but she still knew *Big Blue* wouldn't be there to keep her warm at night, ask her about her day, or bring her roses.

Fine, she didn't really want roses.

Or maybe she did.

At this point, she wasn't sure. All she knew was that there had to be more to life than waking up in the middle of the night, emptying lobster traps, and then making panna cotta and blueberry croissants.

Hours later, she still hadn't worked out the meaning of life, but she felt confident she'd have enough shrimp to satisfy Gwen for the day.

The sun had come up already, and Alissa knew from experience that it was going to be a scorcher of a day. She wiped sweat from her forehead and replaced her disgusting shrimp boat captain hat before texting Gwen to send down her kitchen hands to get all the fish. Long ago, the water had gone almost to the restaurant, and the chutes in the bottom of the boat could be used to get the fish into the kitchen.

But the shoreline had receded a lot over the past few decades, due to more building, more expansion on the island. More wealth. More people discovering the gem of Carter's Cove and booking their family vacations, honeymoons, weddings, anniversaries, and birthday celebrations on the island.

In the summer, the population doubled as tourists poured into town, and yet there always seemed to be enough hotels, enough swimming pools, and enough golf courses to keep everyone happy.

At least Alissa thought so. A new high-rise hotel had started being built just a half a block from her family's land, where they had five homes of various sizes. Alissa didn't share her grandparents' place, but a couple of her sisters shared, with Olympia living full time in the hotel itself.

Theirs was probably the last bit of undeveloped land on the island, though Alissa knew there were wild spots over on the north side too.

Dodger barked as he hit the sand running, and Alissa shaded her eyes as she looked up. Gwen hadn't responded to her text, but she'd obviously gotten it, as several men walked toward them, big, black containers in their hands. Pirate waddled on the sand, and the simple sight of it made Alissa smile.

"Hey, guys," she said, flashing what she hoped was a bright smile at the guys. She thought she was a decent flirt, but none of the kitchen hands had ever asked her out.

That's because Gwen's the cute blonde, Alissa told herself, forcing herself not to turn around and walk backward in the sand. She wasn't a supermodel by any stretch of the imagination, but she liked her curves.

All the right curves in all the right places. At least that was what her mother had always said.

She entered the kitchen through the back door of the restaurant, her calves burning from the long march up the beach. Since she'd thought of blueberry croissants that morning, she hadn't been able to get them out of her head.

But they weren't on her weekly list for the menu, so she couldn't make them. Gwen would have a fit then, and Alissa didn't need the drama in her life. Or maybe she did. Maybe it would be nice to have some drama for a change.

No one bothered her in the pastry nook, and the temperature in the kitchen only increased as the next couple of hours passed. Alissa felt like she'd melt into a puddle of sweat, despite the fan that blew in the corner.

She paused in her work and stepped over to the sink, turning the water on as cold as it would go. Then she practically dunked her head under the stream, the relief to her steamed face instant and refreshing.

"Alissa," Olympia called, and she lifted her head out of the industrial-sized sink.

"Back here."

Her sister's heels clicked toward her, and it wasn't the only pair of footsteps. Alissa couldn't see who she'd brought with her, but it was definitely a man with broad shoulders in one of those annoying polos.

It wasn't even noon yet, and Alissa had no idea what her sister could possibly need from her.

"There you are," Olympia said, as if Alissa had been hard to find.

"Here I am." Her face dripped with water, and she didn't care—until the man stepped out from behind Olympia.

Though she had water droplets clinging to her eyelashes, Alissa could still make out the very handsome face of Shawn Newman.

She sucked in a breath.

The Shawn Newman from her childhood. Teenhood. Whatever.

She searched frantically for a towel, and of course, all such things seemed to have departed the area.

Shawn smiled, and oh, that wasn't fair. He still had that same chestnut hair, those same sparkling blue eyes that had always teased her, even right as he was about to kiss her. Today, he wore a pair of blue board shorts and that blasted polo in lavender, and dang if Alissa's heart didn't beat faster and faster....

It was definitely whole enough for him to break it.

Lavender. She almost scoffed. What kind of man wore lavender?

Shawn Newman, her mind whispered.

"I need you to show Mister Newman around," Olympia said, and alarms sounded through Alissa with the professional, clipped tone of her sister's voice.

"What?" she asked.

"You two were friends in high school, right?" Olympia practically looked down her nose at Alissa, but without those heels, they'd be eye-to-eye.

Friends. Another scoff-worthy word. "Yeah," Alissa said, dragging out the vowels at the end of the word. "Friends."

With benefits, but Shawn just stood there, his winning smile on his face. Alissa wished she wasn't dripping wet and boiling hot. She probably looked like a homeless dog who'd just fallen into pond scum.

"He's back in town for a couple of weeks, and he'll be staying with us," Olympia said. "I've sent you a text with the details of what he needs."

"Why—?"

"Thanks, Liss." Olympia put her fake business smile on her face and turned to Shawn. "She's all yours."

Oh, no she wasn't, and Alissa bristled at the words. At the question her sister had silenced.

Why me?

Alissa didn't deal with high-profile guests. Any of the other sisters would've been a better choice. And she certainly didn't have time for Shawn Newman, his brilliant smile, or the jittery feeling in her stomach.

Oh, Shawn and Alissa are going to be fun! **Read THE HEARTWOOD SEA today - it's available in ebook, paperback, and audiobook!**

The Perfect Storm (Book 1): A freak storm has her sliding down the mountain...right into the arms of her ex. As Eden and Holden spend time out in the wilds of Hawaii trying to survive, their old flame is rekindled. But with secrets and old feelings in the way, will Holden be able to take all the broken pieces of his life and put them back together in a way that makes sense? Or will he lose his heart and the reputation of his company because of a single landslide?

The Overboard Mistake (Book 2): Friends who ditch her. A pod of killer whales. A limping cruise ship. All reasons Iris finds herself stranded on an deserted island with the handsome Navy SEAL...

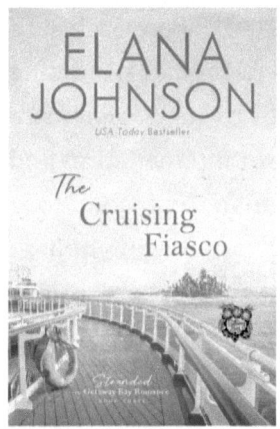

The Cruising Fiasco (Book 3): He can throw a precision pass, but he's dead in the water in matters of the heart...

The Sand Bar Misstep (Book 4): Tired of the dating scene, a cowboy billionaire puts up an Internet ad to find a woman to come out to a deserted island with him to see if they can make a love connection...

BOOKS IN THE GETAWAY BAY
ROMANCE SERIES

The Island House (Book 1): Charlotte Madsen's whole world came crashing down six months ago with the words, "I met someone else."

Can Charlotte navigate the healing process to find love again?

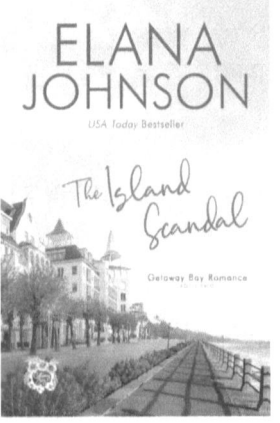

The Island Scandal (Book 2): Ashley Fox has known three things since age twelve: she was an excellent seamstress, what her wedding would look like, and that she'd never leave the island of Getaway Bay. Now, at age 35, she's been right about two of them, at least.

Can Burke and Ash find a way to navigate a romance when they've only ever been friends?

The Island Hideaway (Book 3): She's 37, single (except for the cat), and a synchronized swimmer looking to make some extra cash. Pathetic, right? She thinks so, and she's going to spend this summer housesitting a cliffside hideaway and coming up with a plan to turn her life around.

Can Noah and Zara fight their feelings for each other as easily as they trade jabs? Or will this summer shape up to be the one that provides the romance they've each always wanted?

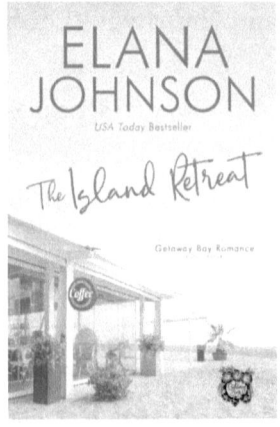

The Island Retreat (Book 4): Shannon's 35, divorced, and the highlight of her day is getting to the coffee shop before the morning rush. She tells herself that's fine, because she's got two cats and a past filled with emotional abuse. But she might be ready to heal so she can retreat into the arms of a man she's known for years...

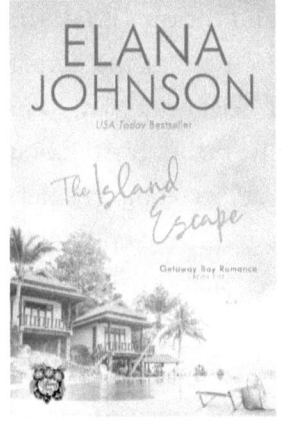

The Island Escape (Book 5): Riley Randall has spent eight years smiling at new brides, being excited for her friends as they find Mr. Right, and dating by a strict set of rules that she never breaks. But she might have to consider bending those rules ever so slightly if she wants an escape from the island...

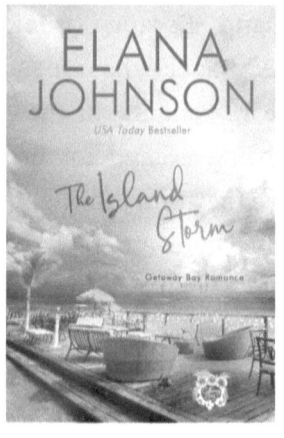

The Island Storm (Book 6):
Lisa is 36, tired of the dating scene in Getaway Bay, and practically the only wedding planner at her company that hasn't found her own happy-ever-after. She's tried dating apps and blind dates...but could the company party put a man she's known for years into the spotlight?

The Island Wedding (Book 7): Deirdre is almost 40, estranged from her teenaged daughter, and determined not to feel sorry for herself. She does the best she can with the cards life has dealt her and she's dreaming of another island wedding...but it certainly can't happen with the widowed Chief of Police.

Aloha Hideaway Inn (Book 1): Can Stacey and the Aloha Hideaway Inn survive strange summer weather, the arrival of the new resort, *and* the start of a special relationship?

Getaway Bay (Book 2): Can Esther deal with dozens of business tasks, unhappy tourists, *and* the twists and turns in her new relationship?

Women's Beach Club (Book 3): With the help of her friends in the Beach Club, can Tawny solve the mystery, stay safe, and keep her man?

Straw and Diamonds (Book 4): Can Sasha maintain her sanity amidst their busy schedules, her issues with men like Jasper, and her desires to take her business to the next level?

The Billionaire Club (Book 5): Can Lexie keep her business affairs in the shadows while she brings her relationship out of them? Or will she have to confess everything to her new friends...and Jason?

Sweet Breeze Resort (Book 6): Can Gina manage her business across the sea and finish the remodel at Sweet Breeze, all while developing a meaningful relationship with Owen and his sons?

Rainforest Retreat (Book 7): As their paths continue to cross and Lawrence and Maizee spend more and more time together, will he find in her a retreat from all the family pressure? Can Maizee manage her relationship with her boss, or will she once again put her heart—and her job—on the line?

Getaway Bay Singles (Book 8): Can Katie bring him into her life, her daughter's life, and manage her business while he manages the app? Or will everything fall apart for a second time?

The Heartwood Sea (Book 1): She owns The Heartwood Inn. He needs the land the inn sits on to impress his boss. Neither one of them will give an inch. But will they give each other their hearts?

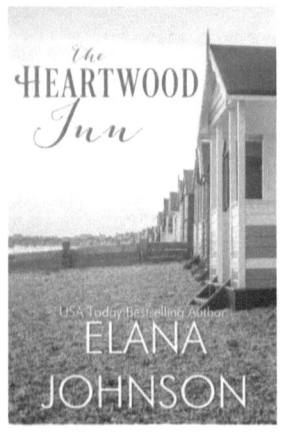

The Heartwood Inn (Book 2): She's excited to have a neighbor across the hall. He's got secrets he can never tell her. Will Olympia find a way to leave her past where it belongs so she can have a future with Chet?

The Heartwood Beach (Book 3): She's got a stalker. He's got a loud bark. Can Sheryl tame her bodyguard into a boyfriend?

The Heartwood Wedding (Book 4): He needs a reason not to go out with a journalist. She'd like a guaranteed date for the summer. They don't get along, so keeping Brad in the not-her-real-fiancé category should be easy for Celeste. Totally easy.

The Heartwood Chef (Book 5): They've been out before, and now they work in the same kitchen at The Heartwood Inn. Gwen isn't interested in getting anything filleted but fish, because Teagan's broken her heart before... Can Teagan and Gwen manage their professional relationship without letting feelings get in the way?

ABOUT ELANA

Elana Johnson is the USA Today bestselling author of dozens of clean and wholesome contemporary romance novels. She lives in Utah, where she mothers two fur babies, works full-time with her husband, and eats a lot of veggies while writing. Find her on her website at feelgoodfictionbooks.com